what i do is
TABOO

The Erotic Series By
YONDER
Volume I

PF and Associates
P.O. Box 2482
Waldorf, Maryland 20604

ISBN: 0-9769772-1-4

Distribution by:
Baker & Taylor and Ingram Book Group

Visit YONDER at www.yonderone.com

Cover and Interior Designed By
The Writer's Assistant
www.thewritersassistant.com

Disclaimer

This book is a work of fiction. Names, characters, places, events, and incidents, are either the product of the author's vivid imagination or are used fictitiously. Any resemblance to actual persons, living or dead is entirely coincidental.

The author or publisher accepts no responsibility for the actions or positions reading this book will produce. It is highly recommended that the reader of this book be in a relationship or at least dating while reading this piece of work.

The contents of these pages are meant to get you hot and bothered.

P.S. Relax and Enjoy. It's Not That Serious!

What I Do Is Taboo

I have sex in public
I will do your wife and girlfriend
I please myself in public restrooms
That's why what I do is Taboo

I have no morals and a big ego
If I get your woman, she will never be yours again
That's why what I do is Taboo

Passion and lust are my specialities. . . one night with me
will even make your thongs blush
That's why what I do is Taboo

The positions i put you in will ease all your stress
and also relieve all your juices
That's why what I do is Taboo

Your wildest fantasies will be fulfilled; your
multi-orgasms will be world class
Your body will crave mine
From now on, you will only desire one thing as if
you're feennin
That one thing is me

That's really why what i do is TABOO

The Multi-Orgasm or the M.O.

Why does the best sex always come from someone that is straight crazy? The bad part about it all is that you know that they're crazy the day you meet them. As the relationship, or should I say the sex-ship goes on, everybody tells you how crazy this person is. You even start seeing the signs yourself, but you're blinded by the sex. The sex is so good your toes curl, your heart knocks, and your dick is like a fire hydrant. The pussy is so wet you feel like you're in the ocean. And don't even mention the multiple orgasms. Have you ever had a *multi* so powerful that you thought you were peeing, having a heart attack, and dying simultaneously? Now that's good sex.

Have you ever ventured to the other side? Have you ever had a multi-orgasm? Would you like to know real satisfaction? Then let's take a ride on the multi side. In order to go, there's only one thing you have to agree to. Before you run and say yes, let me tell you what that one thing is. Are you ready? Can you handle it? Well, here it is: You have to fuck somebody that's crazy, straight loony.

what i do is
TABOO

Maggie's Madness

It was the summer of 1984; this was my second marriage at twenty-two years old. My first husband met an early death. Let's say he was experimenting with it and it eventually happened.

My new husband meant the world to my two daughters and me. He did everything for us, grocery shopping, fixed the girls' hair; I was spoiled. I loved this man. We lived on the northwest side of town in a three-bedroom house; our neighborhood was called the "Gold Coast." My husband owned a plumbing and electrical company, Dickerson Plumbing & Electrical, with twenty-two employees. All my girlfriends were jealous of our status, even my mother hated on me.

But my life changed in 1986. Let me tell you, I grew up poor and unloved, so I felt I needed more. I had two children, which was enough, but I always needed more money, more trips, and more new dick. Let me put it out there, my husband worked so hard that his loving was crap. I needed some youngster to break me down real good so I could go home at night. One day, I was thinking of someone who would be willing to fulfill my needs. That someone was one of my husband's employees. He was six foot three and the women that worked for my husband called him Broom; I always wondered why.

My name is Margaret, but they call me Maggie. I am five foot nine with a pretty face, a nice butt, a small chest, and I consider my pussy the best in the world. I named it Sweetness. My motto was "my sweetness is your weakness." I've always been able to get whatever I wanted from men, so I was cool with me.

Katrina, the receptionist, was the smart one. She was college educated, very conservative, and kind of stout with humongous breasts. She always had a man because she was stable, nothing like most women our age. Rochelle, the secretary, was five foot seven or eight and she wasn't just red, but high yellow and thought she was fine. I really never liked that red girl.

The secretary and receptionist were cool with me, so every now and then we would talk or go out to lunch. Today, the ladies and I went to Timbuktu's in Columbia, Maryland. While we waited for our food, I asked Katrina why they called the tall guy Broom. She replied, "You don't want to know."

We changed the subject when Rochelle returned to the table because she was nosey and close to my old man and I didn't want this conversation to get back to him. We talked about the soaps, make-up, and men. Then Rochelle, the nosey secretary said she had to go to the ladies' room again. Katrina said, "Damn, what's wrong with your booty?" Rochelle blushed and frowned as she walked away.

While I was finishing off my crab cakes and coleslaw, Rochelle returned and we started laughing about her stank booty, saying somebody gave her the vapors. She said, "Let me tell you hoes, if you had what I had you would be smiling."

Katrina and I smiled and said, "You done bumped your head and scratched your clit." That was our favorite saying when a female said something crazy.

what i do is
TABOO

Rochelle said that she would tell a secret if we promised not to tell anyone. Once we agreed she began. "Girls, I had some dick three days ago, the best dick in the world."

Katrina and I started calling out names. "Who, Boo Boo, Raymond, Reggie, who goddamn it?"

She said, "You know the one they call Broom? Well, let me tell you why they call him Broom.

"Broom is short for broomstick. Girls, his stick is thirteen inches long and fat like the end of a baseball bat. I sucked the side of his dick because the head was so big I couldn't get it in my mouth. Was it good! His was so big I could put both hands and mouth on it at the same time. One hand was on each side and my mouth was in the middle, like I was riding a bike and his dick was my handlebars, woooweee.

"He put in all thirteen inches; it was pain before pleasure, like fire and desire. Instead of starting slow he just rammed his dick in and started fucking my brains out. He took a break to lick my ass and I was praying that he didn't want some ass next. Thank God he didn't because I just couldn't take anymore. The pressure of his dick made my legs hurt and after all that action I could barely walk. I had my sister take me to the doctor yesterday. I had to tell him I fell on a broomstick." Rochelle continued. "I told the doctor I was stretching my legs on the wall and came down on the stick part of the broom and couldn't get it out. The doctor gave me some medication for my pussy because the skin had been pulled off. I can't walk straight, girl, but it was well worth it. I can now say that I've had the biggest dick, instead of you, Maggie, bragging about your husband's ten inches."

After hearing all that drama we had to order another round of Blue Hawaiians and we knew no one was going back to the office anytime soon. My panties were soaked just hearing the story and I wanted to know more about Broom.

Let me flow:
> It has been measured – it has been teased,
> It's a treasure to please.
>
> Most want it larger - most claim it is larger.
>
> When it's good it's really good,
> When it's small - it's really sad.
>
> What possesses this power?
> I'm glad you asked.
>
> Broomstick

Pause:
Just the mention of the word dick gets my panties all soaked. I wear briefs almost all the time because I'm always wet and briefs hold my sweet juices in. One time I wore a G-string under my skirt and I was so horny my pussy juice went all down my legs as I was walking. I was really embarrassed so now I keep briefs on at all times.

Let me flow:

> They are worn often,
> Actually too much,
> Their original purpose was not pure,
> They have crossed generations too easily.
>
> They produce pleasure,
> They produce pain.

what i do is
TABOO

The pain is internal,
The pleasure is momentary and visual.

They have even changed the name,
The retailers love these customers.

Customers don't realize,
What this product does to their body.

Even if they did,
Sadly they would still be worn.

Their industry is as powerful as cigarettes, folks.

And secretly I think they have,
Conspired with the drug industry.

I know you think I'm babbling,
And you want to know where I'm going.

Well ladies, pull up your skirts, and drop your pants,
You have them on!

Back to the story:
Friday morning I went to the office early with donuts and pastries. The girls said, "You're really early, Maggie, what's going on?"

I just smiled and blushed; they figured I was up to something. I was wearing a lavender skirt with a split up to my sweetness. But I played it off and told them that I just felt like getting the day started off right. I hung around drinking coffee and talking, waiting on Mr. Broomstick to arrive. As he walked through the door he spoke and flashed his million-dollar grin and went on into the locker room to change into his coveralls. The rest of the guys were waiting in their trucks to begin work.

The ladies were on the phone taking orders and I was waiting for the right time to sneak a peek at this enormous piece of work. As I got closer to the locker room, my husband yelled, "Mag-Mag, what are you doing here this early? You had my employees out all day for lunch yesterday. Are you cutting up again?"

"Dear, I was in the area so I brought the staff some donuts and pastries."

"Thanks Mag-Mag, you sure know what we need." He called the secretary into his office and closed the door.

I was trembling now; I had a real chance to see Broom. I walked up to the locker room, put my hand on the knob, and panicked. I started to get second thoughts: what if he sees me? What if he tells my husband? I lost my courage and sat at the secretary's desk.

When he emerged from the locker room and came to the desk he said, "You're not Rochelle."

I said, "No, but I'm here to help." He grinned and leaned over the desk. My skirt was hiked up, but he didn't even notice my wet pussy sitting there saying TAKE ME NOW.

"What do you need?" I asked.

"It's kind of personal. I know you are the boss' wife and I don't want to offend you, madam."

"You know, my friends call me Maggie."

"Well madam, I'm not your friend, but I need you to deliver a message to Rochelle." I grabbed a pen and paper. He told me that his pants were not fitting properly and that I should take a closer look at how tight they were in the leg. I looked at his coveralls trying to avoid what I really wanted to see. He shook his head and stated, "I don't think you understand, you're looking at my knee." I nodded. "That's not my knee."

He asked me to touch where I thought his knee was so I pushed that spot with my finger. He shook his head and told me that I still didn't understand. Now I was getting pissed because he thought I was stupid. He grabbed my hand and put it where his knee was supposed to be; it wasn't his knee, it was his dick. I pulled back and said, "Hold up, let me do that again." It was rock hard.

I fell out of the chair, my skirt went up, and my panties left a wet mark on the floor. When I got up and composed myself he was gone. I felt ridiculous and horny, so I ran to the ladies' room to relieve myself. I put my leg on the toilet paper holder and started massaging my clit. When I heard the door open I wasn't even close to reaching my peak, so I stopped. I adjusted my clothes, exited the stall, washed my hands, and touched up my hair and make-up. Once outside, I ran full force to my car and pulled out my "Goodie Bag." After a few moments, I realized I really did have some other errands to run, but I wasn't ready to stop pleasing myself or get Broomstick off my mind. I thought, *One last orgasm for the road,* so I starting stroking myself again. Yes, yes, yes, yes, wooooo. I was sweating, my make-up was ruined, and the car seat smelled like my sweetness. My sweetness is also my weakness, girl. I am in love with myself.

Let's pause right there:

What is a **goody bag** you ask? A goody bag is your Emergency Dick Supplies. When you're mad at your mate or he's just not making your toes curl anymore, you pull out the GB. I have three, one in the car, one in the bathroom, and one in the kitchen.

The GB in the kitchen has a clit teaser, lil magic, because it's magic to set a clit on fire. At one time, I only had lil magic, but since my husband stopped tearing this pussy up I had to add a batch of condoms for the fine mailman or UPS man. The GB in the car has another favorite; it's a butt vibrator I call Tim–Tim. I sit on it and drive real fast. Once I was driving over the speed limit and a male police officer pulled me over and asked for my license and registration, and for me to get out of the car. I pleaded with the officer, but he insisted. When I got out of the car he saw that my skirt was hiked up and Tim-Tim was still in my ass. The officer said, "I don't believe this shit." I promptly gave him directions to a side road about a mile away and suggested that we could keep this between us. He agreed and followed me. He came over to my car door and I got on my knees with Tim-Tim still in me and proceeded to suck the skin off his dick. He gave me $100 and drove off. No ticket for me.

Back to the story:
After pleasing myself, I went to pick up some things from the cleaners. I rode up to Nick's Cleaners on Georgia Avenue by Howard University. I parked my car in front of Markie's barbershop, appropriately called "Tighten Up." His business cards read, *If your head ain't tight you need to stop by Tighten Up.* I knew Markie, but he wasn't my type, too big. He was a mixture of Heavy D and Biz Markie.

Pause:
Howard University was like eighty-five percent of all HBCU's in the middle of the hood. Not only did I love coming to the hood for the cleaners, I loved all the young bucks from H.U. trying to get some of my sweetness. There were real people with real issues in the hood, drama style and slang;

what i do is
TABOO

corner stores and barbershops; and beauty salons, churches, and liquor stores on every corner. These may sound like bad things if you're from some uppity, snooty, Ivy League neighborhood, but if you're from the projects, which I was, the hood was good to me. Thank God I'm out of the hood, but the experience was worth it.

Back to the story:
Since I was all horny and feening for some real dick, I put my face on, got myself together, and went into the barbershop. As I strolled in, I smiled at everybody and started some idle chitchat with Markie while he was cutting someone's hair. Markie told the guy he would be back in a minute and asked me to come in the back; he wanted to show me something. I figured he must have some bootleg videotapes or something hot. When I stepped into the back he said, "I don't know how to say this, and don't take this the wrong way, but can I eat you?"

I screamed, "You nasty, fat, Biz Markie-looking motherfucker."

He went back out to the shop and I stood there, actually turned on. Not by Markie's fat ass, but by the thought of getting eaten while all those men were in the other room. I am a true voyeur; I will do it anywhere and I love to be watched.

Pause:
One time I sucked two guys off in the car coming back from a Luther Vandross show. They both paid for the tickets and both received pleasure from my other two lips. They have a nickname also, "the gripper." I don't deep throat, I grip half with my mouth and lick the head one thousand licks a minute, and yes, I swallow.

Side note:

Men, if you want a woman to swallow, change your diet. You are what you eat. Start drinking apple juice, grape juice, and cranberry juice. When a woman knows what she's getting is going to be tasty she will blow you all night for some good cum.

Also shave your pubic area and your ass. I will lick your ass and suck your dick hairless. Hairless – no odor; hair – carries odor. Same for the women: shave that bush. What are you trying to do, put cornrows in it? That's why he never eats you because that pussy stinks. You had that hair since you were twelve; now you know that pussy stank. When an ass is shaved, I will touch it, lick it, and put some whipped cream on it. Whipped cream should be room temperature and flavored. Always use the bowl, not the spray cans.

Back to the story:

I sat in that backroom and started touching myself. Next thing you know, my eyes were closed and I was up on the desk. Before I could say stop, Markie had come in and was on his knees beside the desk licking my sweetness. I said no, but that big fat tongue was huge. I said, "For real Markie, stop!" He stopped for a moment, but then started licking again; he was going so fast I threw my legs around his neck and held on for dear life. I started shaking, screaming, and sweating, and yelled, "Markie, Markie, Markie you the best." And I said it so loudly you could hear it up and down Georgia Avenue. I lost my cool because of my sweetness.

I told you my sweetness is also my weakness. The multi-orgasms kept coming and coming until I was unconscious on the desk. Markie revived me by saying the typical male nonsense, "Whose is it?" and I could do nothing but reply,

what i do is
TABOO

"It's yours, Markie." I came back to my senses after saying that, but not before I could see the curtains moving, eyes peeping.

THE END

Feening In the Summer Of 1988

The dictionary defines feening as: addicted to, can't get enough, and habit forming...Modern culture describes feening as whipped, hooked, no control, and junkie. I describe feening as good pussy.

It was the summer of 1988; I was at The Point. Every town has a park that everybody hangs at; in Philly it's called The Plateau and in my hometown of DC it's called Haines Point. I was at The Point hanging with everybody, from hustlers to ballers (or wannabe ballers), and all the honeys. On any given day, from Easter Sunday until it got cold around late October, The Point would be packed. You could get in on any weekday, but on the weekends you had to be in before noon or the gates would be locked. Some days there would be hundreds of cars with booming systems and the motorcycle crews would be in full force.

This one weekend, I had on some fly gear and my EK sunglasses. You had to have some EK's to be allowed at The Point. The fellas and I were having a good time watching the ladies and drinking Lowenbrau. I drove a Maxima with five star rims; my partner, Dre, drove a candy-apple red Toyota Cressida with a kit; my other partner, Darnell, drove a Suzuki Jeep with a speaker system so loud it could blow your eardrums. There was something strange about this day because Dre was getting all the play, even though he wasn't a lady's man. He liked the ladies, but never knew what to say to them. Darnell and I were the real playas, but we weren't getting any play.

what i do is
TABOO

I was shooting the breeze with some of the fellas from Barry Farms when I saw her. She was six feet tall, had long hair down her back like an Indian, a caramel complexion mixed with a little bit of chocolate, and long brown legs with a gap to die for. This girl was located under "fine" in the dictionary. And check this out; she was a virgin. That's right; probably the last one on earth, 'cause this was the eighties and everybody was getting broke off.

This young lady was truly playing hard to get. She told me her name was Tessa; I told her my name was Courtney, but they called me Mr. Roarke like on Fantasy Island.

"Why do they call you Mr. Roarke?"

My response was, "Wouldn't you like to know?" One of my partners paged me, so I found a payphone, but when I came back she was gone. I said, "Damn, now that could have been the one; I could have made her my main lady." Since Tessa and I only exchanged names I didn't know how to get in contact with her. I was pissed; Mr. Roarke couldn't get what he wanted.

Pause:

The reason I have so many women is because I have special needs. I love a specialist - a specialist is a person that's good at one thing. These are the names of the specialists: Psychologist (head doctor) if she gives superb head. Gynecologist (pussy doctor) gynee for short if the pussy is the bomb. Proctologist (ass doctor) pro for short if she has a big ass and lets you go through the back door. It was very rare when you would find a girl with all the degrees; she would be called an M&M or Mother Material. She was real good, but you considered her old.

Remember, I'm only twenty-two, but the times that I had an M&M it was the bomb. She washed you up, sexed you up, fed you, and paid you. That's the life.

Back to the story:
That night we went to a lawn party in Maryland and everybody was there. There were three go-go bands, rappers Doug E. Fresh and Biz Markie, and a DJ from Barry Farms, DJ Juicy, the best DJ on the east coast and one of my boys. As I walked the yard, I felt this was going to be one of those nights. I could feel The Zone coming around me and I was in my element. I was the main event, the main attraction. When you looked for me you looked for action. That's enough of me blowing my own horn; later on tonight I will have someone else blowing it for me.

What's The Zone?
Let me give you the lowdown on The Zone. The Zone is a special place most men and women only reach maybe twice in their entire lifetime. Most don't even know what The Zone is.

Zoners - Once you enter The Zone more than twice you are known as a zoner.

Let me give you the details. The Zone is when everything you say and do is what everyone else would love to say and do. I can briefly describe it as everything you touch turns to gold. When a man has mastered The Zone society can't understand the magic he possesses, but as men do with everything, we abuse it. We will do your mother, your sister, your aunt, your niece, and anyone else that falls in the way while we're there.

Yes, women also use The Zone. There have been a few women I know to manipulate The Zone so well that they have luxury cars to prove it. And yes, they have reversed the game to make men into psychologists. Oh yes, women love for men to give them head or eat them. The Zone is mastered by both sexes.

what i do is
TABOO

Back to the story:

There were ladies from uptown, Morgan, North Carolina, A&T, and the hood. As I gave the peace sign and what's up to B.F. and V.G., I pulled up to a redbone. Even though I couldn't stand redbones, I knew she would be easy for my first number of the night. She was actually a knockout and her name was Kitty. She was strictly tits and ass, which was good, but not my type. I'm six feet, dark-skinned, and most redbone girls love me, but I like dark-skinned girls. I could walk around with $500 in a Ziploc bag stuck to my chest and dark-skinned girls still wouldn't holla at me. But a redbone would see me a thousand miles away and give me the world.

I started talking to the redbone, saying one of my corny pick-up lines. "You're as cute as a button." She blushed and asked my name. I told her they call me Mr. Roarke. We walked over to the bar, got a drink, and I saw another young lady waving me over. The redbone thought she said something worthwhile, but my mind was in this other girl's panties. I excused myself and went to the men's room so I could get a closer look at this honey waving me over. I could tell from a distance that she was fine, but I had to get a closer look since I'd been drinking. Alcohol could play games with your eyes.

Pause:

ALCOHOL - One time I had too much to drink and did this girl. When I woke up the next morning she was so ugly I had to beat her ass. But it was some good pussy. It talked, walked, gripped, and sang my name all night. She gave me head and inhaled everything including my balls and licked my ass. Her tongue was longer than my dick and she had skills. I get excited just talking about her. Fellas and ladies, if you want some not just good, but some terrific fucking, get an ugly man or woman. You will be thanking me the next day.

This girl was so good I had to share her with my boys. I did apologize for beating her up. She sucked three of us at the same time and we were giving each other high-fives. Then she told us all to grab a hole. I stayed with the mouth and my other two partners went front and back door. She had us all screaming in ecstasy. She also burnt all of us so we were singing Kool Moe Dee's, *Go See the Doctor* as we went to get cured.

Three days later we woke up pussing and cussing. Remember this was the eighties. You could get some penicillin and call it a day. When you get burnt in the hood, you went to Dr. Black on MLK Avenue. His office was up the street from the Big Chair in apartment building number 8A. It was always crowded with hustlers, honeys, children, and STD victims. My crew had been burnt so much we just kept the penicillin bottle and just got it refilled. When Dre or Darnell needed it they would call me and I would laugh first, then ask the girl's name, and give them the bottle and the Kool Moe Dee tape.

Back to the story:

I actually did have to take a leak, so after I came out of the bathroom, I went over to the honey that was waving me over. She was about five foot two with a beige complexion and a short tight Anita Baker hairdo. She was short but thick with no chest or waist, just big thighs and ass for days. I like short girls because you can make their bodies do all sorts of things. Like this one girl I used to date, I would sit her on top of me and spin her around like a top.

As I was talking to shorty, the redbone came over. I said, "Hey, Boo," because I never remembered names. She immediately had an attitude.

"Roarke, I see you still in the bathroom, huh?"

I was about to walk away then I said to myself, *Hey you, in The Zone, you can make this work in your favor.* So I introduced the girls. "Boo this is Shorty." Shorty said her name was Michele Stevens. I started talking to them as if they were best friends and came to the party together. (You can only do this if you are in The Zone.) As we were conversing, I thought I would do something. In Michele's ear I whispered, "Do you like to be eaten?" In Tonya's ear I whispered, "Do you like to cum?" They both replied, "Yes!" I wanted a *ménage-à-trois* or for hood folks, a good ole threesome. We had some more drinks and they seemed ready and willing. Then it happened. I couldn't believe it. I put my drink down and tried to clear my head. I don't believe in fate, but I had to compose myself so I went back to the men's room. Mr. Roarke was actually nervous; Tessa was here.

The DJ started playing some old school so everybody was dancing, getting his or her groove on. Tonya and Michele pulled me onto the yard and started to freak me. They were playing one of my favorites, this joint by Tom Brown called *Jamaica Funk.* I loved that jam so I had to show off some of my moves. Then they started mixing some P-FUNK with Holy Ghost by the Barkays. DJ Juicy was blowing up the spot. He pulled out some of Chuck Brown's *Bustin' Loose* and I was doing my thing. When I came back to my senses, I excused myself to go holla at my boy Dre. He told me that Tessa was over by the pool. When I ran over there lo and behold she was in the pool in a two-piece bikini. There had to be at least twenty fellas at the pool just slobbering from the mouth just looking at her. She paid no attention to me. I was pissed so I went and got a drink.

The DJ was pumping up the volume on the party when he turned it over to Rare Essence. Once Essence got on I told myself that I wasn't going to sweat her. Who did she think she was? Mr. Roarke don't sweat nobody. I went back to the bandstand and Essence started jamming. The first beat was the roll call and the band said my name first. Yes, I was still in

The Zone. I waved for Michele and Tonya to come over, and of course they ran. I didn't miss a beat. We started talking and dancing again. I was wearing a silk short set and after rubbing up against Tonya my manhood was hanging out. Michele saw it out and started to rub it with her hand. Tonya started to put her ass on Michele's hand as she rubbed me. The Zone is special. I was about to make my exit and get this party started right. I waved over to Dre and Darnell, pulled them to the side, and told them I was on my way to Crystal City and I was going solo tonight. Darnell said, "Damn Roarke, you selfish."

I told Darnell, "It's all zone baby and I'm in it." As we walked to my car, Dre gave me props; he yelled out, "Roarke, you the man," then Darnell yelled, "That's my motherfucking boy." I held up the peace sign and we were out.

Crystal City is a town that has several hotels and when you have a certain caliber of honey you step it up a notch. I stopped at the liquor store on the way to a Holiday Inn and picked up some wine coolers, honeys love coolers. As we approached the hotel, I couldn't shake the thought of Tessa. I went in to get the room. The clerk was fine; she asked if it would be all right to check in on me to make sure the room was in tip-top shape. I said, "As fine as you are, you can check in on me now." I went back to the car to let the ladies know that we were in room 524 and I told them to come up separately, about five minutes apart.

I grabbed my duffle bag and went up to the room. My duffle bag had all sorts of gels, lotions, candles, and a small cassette player with tapes of Luther and Teddy P. Since I had stepped up my game I also had some Jodeci, Diary of a Mad Band. That tape was off the hook, guaranteed to get you some butt.

When I got to the room, I got into the shower and about ten minutes later, Tonya came in followed shortly by Michele.

what i do is
TABOO

Yes, I was living every man's dream. While we were giggling and lathering each other up with the soap, I noticed Michele was eyeing Tonya's ass; it was perfect. I whispered in Michele's ear, "I dare you to touch it." Tonya was under the water with her back to us. I touched her first and got no response, but when Michele touched it, Tonya responded with an "Ooh." My dick said, "It's on." I got out of the shower and went into the room to set up. I took out the candles, lit some incense, opened three wine coolers, and plugged in the cassette player with Teddy P. playing first.

When I walked back into the bathroom, Tonya had Michele on the toilet, legs opened, licking her like an ice-cream cone. I got so turned on I couldn't move; they didn't notice me standing there with my dick harder than eighty-five boxes of jawbreakers. I dropped to my knees behind Tonya and started banging her from behind. She was so wet. It was good stuff and I had to adjust myself more than twice, so I suggested we take the party to the bed.

The lights were off in the room and all you could see were the heart-shaped candles around the bed. Teddy P. was singing, *Come On and Go With Me;* the mood was set. They got onto the bed and resumed and I was again behind Tonya and yes it was on. I was pounding Tonya's ass and everyone was saying ooh, ahh, and then out of nowhere Michele started screaming and shaking. Tonya and I got scared because we had never seen this before; she shook and screamed for about five minutes then she blacked out. Me being selfish said to myself, *The one time I can have a threesome and one of the honeys is going to die on me.* As Michele started to come to, she laughed at us. "You don't know what just happened. I passed out 'cause I've been on the other side."

Tonya asked, "What other side?"

Michele explained that she'd had a multi-orgasm and then she taught us how to give and receive them. I knew how to give them, but I didn't know that I could have one. I was blown away and so was Tonya. We left the hotel two days later.

My pager was blowing up the whole weekend from Dre, Darnell, and my mother. I saw my mother Monday morning as I was going into the house; she was leaving for work. Yes, I lived at home with my mother.

Pause:

Most playas learn their skills from their mother. My mother taught me how to handle women in any situation and taught me how to manipulate them to get what I wanted. So women, when a guy tells you he's tight with his mother, just remember that he's learning how to take advantage of you.

Back to the story:

My mother told me to call her at work later. When I called she said, "Boy, I been calling you all weekend. Where you been?" I told her about my weekend at the Holiday Inn and she said, "You and those hoes. One day you're going to get one that's going to treat you like you treat them and then she's going to leave you hanging." I told my mother about Tessa and that she just did something to me, she gave me this warm and fuzzy feeling when I first met her and I've never felt that way before. And then when coincidence put us back together at the party, I knew something special would develop. "Something special?" she replied. "I know you're not talking about marriage or children, you too young."

"Not yet, I just want one special lady and I'm getting tired of my playa status."

When she realized that I was serious, she said, "I want to talk more about this later. Be home by five tonight."

After hanging up with Mom, I went to Iverson Mall to get some sneakers and then to Sam's Carwash. No matter what time of day you went to Sam's it was always packed. To kill some time I rode out to Landover Mall. This was the hot spot; you could always see a few hundred folks out there. By four o'clock I was on my way home with my new outfit and a clean ride. When Mom got in she told me she wanted to go out to dinner at Chesapeake Bay Seafood House.

The only girls that get to eat at Chesapeake were your mother or grandmother. If you brought a girlfriend to the Chesapeake she had to be special or be paying for it. As I drove, we discussed Tessa. I told her that there was something soothing about her presence and it kind of bothered me, but I liked it anyway. These were some weird feelings for me. You know certified playas like myself don't get attached; we break them off and go onto the next challenge.

The parking lot was packed and Mom didn't want to wait any longer than thirty minutes for a table. I made my way up to the front of the line and saw this honey that had been sweatin' me for about a year. I used to mess with her girlfriend, Melissa, and her girlfriend told her about me. When I got to her I said, "You don't remember me do you?"

She seemed nervous. "They call you Mr. Roarke, right?"

I asked her name. "Simi Nita, but they call me Simi." She said she was the assistant manager.

"I'm here with my mom, could you do something to get us in?" I asked.

She said, "Of course, but you have to take my phone number and give me your pager number."

I asked what she was going to do if I called. She said that she would do everything that Melissa wouldn't. I whispered in her ear, "Are you a freak?"

She pulled me close. "I will do you tonight." I told her to page me.

I went back to get my mother. "You know I always got an ace in the hole, come with me." As we walked into the restaurant and sat down, Mom said, "Boy, you do use your power don't you?"

As we got settled the waitress came to introduce herself as Shenika. She took our drink orders, lemonade for Mom and a Miller for me. The waitress came back with our drinks and the world famous hushpuppies. Mom asked me to tell her more about Tessa. As I started to describe her, I got that feeling again. I looked over toward the ladies' room and whom do I see? It was like time had stopped. Tessa strolled out of the ladies' room like a runway supermodel.

It wasn't like me to lose my cool, but that Jodeci song, *I Can't Leave You Alone You Got Me Feening,* started playing in my head. We locked eyes and then she turned her head and walked the other way. I continued my conversation with Mom and watched Tessa until she was seated. I wanted to know who brought her here. I went to the men's room and as I walked by I saw her table. She was with two guys and a young lady. It looked like a double date. As I was washing my hands, one of the dudes from her table came in and I said, "Wassup?"

He replied, "That chick out there is trippin'."

"What you mean brotha?"

He said, "She keeps talking about some other dude named Roarke."

"What? She's talking about some other dude? Man, I wouldn't take that."

"You're right; let me go handle this business."

I hid the smile on my face as I gave him a pound and went back to my table. Tessa waved at me. Mom wanted more information and I explained how I felt each time I saw her, how my heart started to pump faster, how I got all nervous, checking the mirror to see that my haircut was tight and there was nothing in my teeth; stuff like that.

My mother said, "Baby, that's just infatuation; you are infatuated because she pays no attention to you and secretly that turns you on. If she started treating you like everyone else you wouldn't act like this."

Then I said, "Hold up, Mom, clarify this again. When she starts paying attention to me I'll get bored like I do with the rest of the girls I meet?"

Pause:

I am a Gemini by birth and also by nature. I am not only a twin, but there are probably ten different personalities going on inside me on any given day. Gemini's get bored with everything and everybody. This is how I would describe most people born under this zodiac sign, especially myself. Exciting, sensual, energetic, crazy, and freaky, we are world-renowned lovers, but our partners must never let us become bored. We are lovable, likable, fantastic talkers, and love warriors. To keep us satisfied one must allow us to be free to be ourselves, whichever personality or freak we are at the time.

Back to the story:

As I tune back into the restaurant scene, I hear some commotion coming from Tessa's table, then I see her and her girlfriend walking to the door alone. I got up to ask them if everything was all right, even though I already knew that it wasn't. Her girlfriend looked upset, but Tessa said they were all right. I asked if they wanted to sit at my table and have some dinner. Tessa said sure, but her girlfriend, Mita, said, "We don't know you like that for you to be feeding us, what you want, some pussy for some crab legs? We don't roll like that, whatever they call you Mr. Roy, Mr. Rich, or Mr. Asshole; we're going home. We've had enough of sorry ass men for the night!"

Tessa whispered to Mita to chill out and stated that a real man would like to treat us to dinner. Eventually Mita agreed to stay even though I wished she had gone home alone. I can't stand a loud mouth woman with a ghetto tongue, always cursing. My mother always said that women who cursed all the time were called "Alley Cats," which meant the bottom of the barrel. I tried my best to stay away from that caliber of woman or at least not bring them home.

I told Tessa and Mita that they had to agree to one thing before dinner. Mita said, "I told you he wants a blow job or a hand job."

I said, "No, I don't roll like that. Be nice to the young lady that's sitting at the table already."

"You're asking us to eat with you and you already have a date?"

"It's not like that, this very special woman is my mother."

Mita whispered to Tessa, "If you don't holla at him I will. A brotha that takes his mother out to dinner, even if it's not a special occasion, is a fine man to me."

Tessa agreed. As we walked back to the table along came another one of those songs, *So You Having My Baby and It Means So Much To Me*. I'm losing my cool again, but I'm trying to hold on.

We sat down and I did the introductions. "M this is Mita and Tessa." Everyone called my mother "M." I motioned to the waitress and she came over to take Mita's and Tessa's orders and returned with more hushpuppies. When the waitress returned she asked if Mita and Tessa were at another table with two guys. They said yes and the waitress told them that the other guys walked out without paying. Before she could finish Mita jumped up and said, "Bitch, you don't know us!" M advised Mita that that wasn't the way to handle the situation and took her to the ladies' room to calm her down. I excused myself, found the manager, and explained the situation, I also requested a new waitress. Never get your server mad at you;

you don't know what they'll put in your food.

M brought Mita back to the table and the manager came over to apologize for the waitress' behavior.

Since all was well, M started asking Mita a few questions: did she have any children, did she work or was she in college? Mita responded no, she did not have any children and that she was in college. M then moved on to Tessa, asking her if she was interested in me and was she a virgin. Tessa responded that she thought that I was mysterious and that it turned her on. The answer to the second question was that she was a virgin and proud of it. At that moment everyone paused including the waitress who had just brought our food. It was as if time stood still. My dick immediately got hard.

Pause:

I never had a virgin. Ooh, this is going to be so sweet, I can't wait. My mind is telling me the V; she will worship me, kiss the ground I walk on, even drink my bath water. My imagination is taking over all sense of reality: Shoop, let a man dream.

Back to the story:

As we ate I had this smile on my face daydreaming about Tessa and me getting married. *Hold up, Roarke, you haven't gotten the drawers yet.* M caught me smiling and asked why Tessa and me were wearing that silly grin. I responded I was just daydreaming. Tessa said that she was smiling because she appreciated the true gentleman that I was by rescuing her out of harm's way. "That's a real man in my eyes, madam."

"That's right, I raised a real man." Then M started to toot my horn by stating that I was educated, mannered, had a good government job, and was working on opening my own consulting firm. "And to top it off the boy is fine. Don't y'all agree, ladies?" she asked. They both nodded in agreement. Now I was pumped; my head was as big as the restaurant, but then M pulled me back down to earth. "Don't let this go to your head, son." The ladies laughed.

When the check arrived I paid the waitress. I asked Tessa and Mita if they needed a ride home and they agreed. I told them that I had to take M home first. When we got to the car, I opened the doors for all the ladies. Mita and Tessa were eating this up in the backseat. They were whispering stuff like, "You better holla at him or I will." I turned on Grover Washington Jr. "Mr. Magic" and pulled off.

When I got to my street, M asked that I not double-park, but find a parking space and pull in. As I backed into the space, M turned around and told the girls that she would like to get to know them better. M told them about the cookout on the third Saturday of the month and asked that they come and bring a few of their friends with them. The girls were thrilled and M hugged them as they got out and changed seats. I asked Tessa to come up front and she gave me directions to Mita's.

Mita came around to my side of the car and thanked me for dinner. She whispered in my ear, "I swallow," and I laughed. Then she grabbed my face and tongue kissed me. I pushed her away, but wondered, *Would she give it to me tonight?* I loved one-night stands.

Tessa told Mita to stop acting like a hoe. "That's why you can't keep a man. You give up the goodies too early." Mita swished her hips left and right and I watched her until she entered the house. The first thing that went through my mind was, *These Maryland chicks don't know what they are about to get themselves into.* Even though I'd had a good upbringing from my mother, I was straight hood; I was a hoe to the utmost. In the dictionary under the word freak, there

what i do is
TABOO

was a picture of me with three women in handcuffs on their knees serving me.

Side note:

I love one-night stands. I had a one-night stand years ago and the pussy was so good she became my main girlfriend. Yes, I admit it; she was a redbone. She had big titties before they were in fashion. Thirty-eight triple D's to be exact. With a small waist and a cute face, ooh, I have visions of her often.

Back to the story:

Tessa asked me if she could listen to the radio and turned it to WHUR. Melvin Lindsey was playing Chapter 8, *I Just Wanna Be Your Girl.* I started singing to Tessa and she started singing back to me. I was thinking, *Heaven must be like this,* and I started to wonder if this was real. All sorts of new thoughts were going through my mind, like, *Is she the one?* And the one thought every playa hates to think: *Do I love her?*

Tessa whispered in my ear that she wasn't ready to go home. I asked where she wanted to go and what she would like to do. She told me to decide and I started to think about all the secluded spots I could take her to. It was about eighty degrees, so of course The Point would have been nice, but it would be crowded. I wanted to take her to Anacostia Park, but that was where everybody went to get his or her freak on and I didn't want to give her the wrong impression. Then I thought about Saint Elizabeth's. This was a spot that only a few people knew about located on a hill with a nice view of DC and the moon on a clear night. This was the place to go on the Fourth of July. White folks went to the monument to watch fireworks. In the city, black folks went to St. E's and the Panorama Room on Morris Road.

When we got to St. E's, I opened the sunroof and reclined our seats. She asked where we were. "It's my little hideaway," I replied.

"Do you bring all your female friends here?"

"No, this is my first time being here with a woman. I usually come here alone to sort things out peacefully."

She leaned over to face me. "What type of things?"

"Sometimes life is not fair." She put her finger over my lips and kissed me. Tessa's lips were so tender, my hands started to roam her fine legs, as we tongued each other down. "It's about to be on." I slowed down to enjoy the moment. I stopped the kissing and we got out of the car to walk down the hill. I ran back to my car and grabbed the cooler, my duffle bag, and a blanket. I always had to set the mood. We sat on the blanket with a few candles, she drinking a cooler and me with my Lowenbrau, looking up at the moon. What a position: Tessa, the moon, and me.

We stayed at St. E's until one thirty in the morning. I was in the process of deciding how to ask her to be my lady, when she asked me if she could be my one and only. My mouth wouldn't open, so she asked again, as if I didn't hear her the first time. Before I could answer she said that she knew about my past. "My past? What about my past?"

She told me that she knew Michele, Candice, Melinda, and at least fifty other women that I've dated. "A lot of the women spoke very highly of your bedroom manner. Although you did dog them out, you were tender and always made them feel like they were number one. Candice actually, gave me play-by-play details of how you ate her out and then made love to her. They all expressed your most worthy talent and that's the talent I want to be used on me." She continued. "You're the only one that made them have a multi-orgasm and I have been dreaming about multi-orgasms all my adult years."

what i do is
TABOO

Tessa had the body of a model. I started to caress her nipples and when she put her hand on my thigh she was surprised to find my dick was already out. As the kisses and caressing got heavier, I put my hand up her mini-skirt. She wasn't wearing panties; my, she sure felt good. I haven't even gotten in yet and my dick felt like it was about to explode. I slowed down and turned her around so I could massage her clit and we could see the stars. I told you I set the mood. She started to moan and purred like a kitten; suddenly my hand was filled with her juices. She apologized and seemed to be embarrassed, but once she composed herself, she said, "I've never felt that way before." My ego was telling me to say something, but my emotions told me to just stroke her. I went straight to her inner thighs to tell her how special I thought she was when she blurted out, "Take me, right here, right now." Here comes that Jodeci song again, *So You Having My Baby and It Means So Much To Me.*

I whispered in her ear that I didn't want to fuck her, I wanted to make love to her and when I finished with making the mood right she would know it. I wanted her to know how special she was to me.

On Tuesday morning, I was at work sitting at my desk when I received a call from security that someone was at the front desk to see me. When I got there Tessa was sitting at the desk. She stood and said, "I need to frisk you for weapons." I immediately got excited and she noticed the bulge in my pants. "Is that a gun in your pocket or are you just happy to see me?" We both laughed and embraced.

"What are you doing here and where is the security guard?" She said the security guard took a break and that she could do whatever she wanted with whomever she wanted to do it with. Later I would hate that statement.

When Officer Bryant returned, I said, "OB, how'd she get you to leave your post?"

"Roarke, that young lady has a way with words." OB pulled me to him and whispered what she had said she wanted to do to me. "I was excited for you, man."

I walked Tessa back to her car and told her to meet me in front of the building. When I got back to my office I told my supervisor, Mrs. Thomas, that I needed to step out for a few hours, but that I would be back. My supervisor was like a mother figure; as long as she knew where you were it was all right. I loved this job and especially Mrs. Thomas.

I met Tessa at the front door; she had turned on an Anita Baker song, *I Just Wanna Be Your Girl.* She asked if I wanted to drive. I told her no, but I suggested we cruise through Georgetown. We went to Sequoia's, an outdoor cafe. I ordered the seafood special and Tessa ordered a fish sandwich; I started teasing her by saying, "Don't try to kiss me with that fishy breath."

She laughed. "You had no problem kissing these lips last night. The next time you kiss these lips you'll have to kiss these first."

I looked under the table and saw that she wasn't wearing any panties and her pussy lips looked so tasty. There was a long tablecloth on our table, so I got under the table and licked her pussy for a few seconds and then returned to my seat. She begged me to finish her off, but I told her we had to eat lunch first. The waitress returned with our food and drinks. While we ate, Tessa put her feet in my lap and massaged my dick. I told her that she was bold to be a virgin. She said that she had always been an avid reader of Harlequin Romance novels and her mother's Forum magazine, which had all sorts of naughty tales. Tessa said she also used to sneak her daddy's Playboy magazines. She had been reading about making love for so long that now she wanted to do it.

After lunch we walked the waterfront toward the shops along the hiker/biker paths. I motioned her over to the side and started to kiss her. She pulled away from me and pulled my zipper down. When my zipper came down, my dick popped out. She stood back. "Wow, it's even bigger than last night." She got on her knees. "I've wanted to do this for a long time." She started giving me head and I was helpless.

I stopped her and told her this wasn't the place. "You'll get your chance, just not here in the woods. When I break you in it will be special."

We left the park and went back to her car. She was pissed and I explained again that the right time was near. As she drove out of Georgetown, I suggested we go to The Point and she agreed. It was about five o'clock in the evening and her girlfriend Mita was there. I saw some fellas from uptown and two old girlfriends.

Once we found a place to park, I went to the men's room. When I returned, I heard Mita and some of her girls at the car talking to Tessa. "How was it? Is it as good as they say? Did you have a multi?"

As I got closer to Tessa, I grabbed her and tongued her down; they all looked at her with envy. Her friend Patrice said, "So y'all all in love now, huh?"

Someone else started to laugh. "How long is this going to last? You know his track record."

So I kissed her again and by the time we came up for air everybody was sitting at the tables. We walked over hand in hand and Mita said to her girlfriends, "I guess they're an item now."

I had big plans for Tessa and me for the weekend. I made reservations at the Embassy Suite Hotel and dinner reservations at an exclusive restaurant in Crystal City that overlooks Virginia and DC.

After dinner we went to the suite and I ordered some Dom Perignon; I had to have champagne to set it off. The sitting room was also laid out with rose petals leading to the bedroom. Tessa got into the shower first and came out with this sexy pink negligee. When I got out of the shower, I popped the champagne and we toasted to the night. I got a bottle of white wine from my cooler and laid her down on the bed. I poured wine all over her and then licked her dry. I took out the whipped cream to get it to room temperature and pulled out a bag of chocolate kisses. I inserted the kisses in her as I licked the rest of her body. I started to slowly lick her clit and soon the chocolates started to melt and slowly dripped out of her. I loved it when a plan came together. I started eating the chocolate from her pussy and added the whipped cream; she was delicious. She tasted better than Baskin Robbins, Carvel, and Haagen-Dazs combined. This pussy was the bomb.

Since I knew she was a virgin, she needed a lot of foreplay. Fellas, if you want total satisfaction from a woman, spend some quality time at foreplay. She will stay moist and in the mood all night. I had my hand in her and she was so ready. I positioned myself at the end of the bed and pulled her down to the edge. I put her long legs over my shoulders and entered her; she was moist, but still tight. Actually it was hurting me more than her. The head of my dick is the size of a doorknob, so entry is usually hard for me. I didn't want to hurt her, so I went in inch-by-inch, slowly, slow, slow; aah, the head is in.

I made sweet love to her and told her how special she was. As the night went on she asked me to try some other positions; I was so willing. There was a chair by the window and I motioned her to it. I sat down and had her sit on top of me. She wrapped her legs around me; it felt really good. I turned her around to ride me backward so I could go deeper. Lifting her legs higher she started yelling, "It's so damn good," and then we fell out of the chair and into each other's arms laughing.

what i do is
TABOO

While we were on the floor, I began again; she was in pure ecstasy. By arching her up slightly I had control of her every movement. Next I stood her up, put one of her legs on my shoulder, and leaned her against the wall. She was crying, "Don't stop, it feels so good." I finally came and we lay on the bed sweaty and tired.

At about two o'clock in the morning I woke her up with my tongue. She started smiling and breathing heavy until she reached her peak. "Mr. Roarke, make my fantasies come true. I hope this weekend never ends."

I asked her to sit up and began to tell her how special this past week had been. "Let me say it's been out of this world. I just want to, I just want to ask you to be my one and only."

She said, "Of course, but will you be my one and only also?"

I said, "Yes," and we embraced and started making love again. I finally reached my peak and it was a multi. I closed my eyes and woke up to a pleasant surprise; Tessa giving me head. Life is sweet when you're me. I'm ready again, but let her continue.

I asked her if I could put her in a position that men only dreamed of. "I'm willing to do anything to please you, Roarke."

I told her that it would hurt, but once she adjusted her body she would feel fine. "Just close your eyes and trust me." She complied and I positioned myself and told her to take two deep breaths. After the first breath I put one leg behind her head, and as she exhaled and took a second breath, I put her other leg behind her head. She looked like a pretzel.

She opened her eyes and yelled, "What the hell are you doing? You're a freak. Who would do some strange stuff like this?"

I said, "Relax and enjoy." I took my time and sat her on top of me backward and then I went to town.

"Stop, stop, it hurts." I slowed down but went deeper; her body reacted and started to spit out all these juices. Now she was talking trash. "This is some good pussy, isn't it? This is the best you ever had, say it Roarke, this pussy is the bomb." You wouldn't have thought this virgin had it in her. Well now, who's in control? "Fuck me," she said, "fuck me harder and claim this pussy. Whose pussy is it?"

Now I was yelling, "It's mine, it's mine." She had me actually crying. This wasn't what a playa was supposed to do. Real playas don't roll like that. I put her on the bed and started licking her back. I was getting her moist and loose. I grabbed the wine and splashed it on the hole, and then I grabbed the whipped cream, put it on my finger and slipped it in, then another, and another until all four fingers were in her ass, but it was still tight. I knew she wasn't ready but she was yelling at me. "Damn it, Roarke, put it in." I told her I was going to take my time, but my dick was in control; it had a mind of its own. I tried to take it easy, but I rammed her. She screamed, "Put it in or take it out." I put a pillow over her mouth and shoved it in. The pussy started farting and the ass started to adjust. When I took the pillow off she yelled, "Fuck me, fuck me good."

I had one more surprise position in mind. Picture this: I lie down on my back and put two pillows under my head so I could brace myself. She stands up and then sits on my dick like you would sit in a chair. This puts her in total control of penetration and she can go down as far as she can handle.

Pause:

Once I had a young lady that could put her legs behind her head in a pretzel position, but she could not get them down. I would do her the whole weekend. I would go outside, wash my car, come back, tap it again, go to the club, come home

four hours later, and hit it again. She would be stuck until I
released her. Yes, I was cruel, but it was so good having
complete control of her every movement.

Back to the story:

We slept until six o'clock that evening. I woke her so we
could take a shower and get something to eat. "Damn, you
fucked me so good I missed two meals and didn't realize it.
Most women would say you fucked the shit out of them, but
not me, I can say you fucked me so good I forgot to eat.
Roarke, you are truly the man and as for that ass stuff, even
though I enjoyed it, I can't take that no more. I feel like shit is
about to run out of my ass. I can probably fit an apple in there
now."

We stopped at Ollie's Trolley, a little hamburger joint
that had some good burgers and fries. The fries were seasoned
with a special salt that made them irresistible, better than
McDonald's. We took the food back to the hotel, but when
we got back, I got this sense that people were looking at us.
"Do you know any of these people?" Tessa asked.

When I got to our suite, I noticed the message waiting
light blinking on the phone. I called the front desk and told
her my name and room number. She asked me to come to the
front desk. "I just have a few questions for you, sir."

I told Tessa I was going to the front desk and would be
right back. When I got to the lobby, there were about ten
people waiting for me at the front desk and they asked me to
follow them.

Once in the room they asked me to sit down. "What's
this is all about?" I questioned.

They all smiled and one young lady blurted out, "What
were you doing to that girl last night? We got complaints about

screams from your room all night. Each time we sent someone up to check it out they all came back saying the girl was screaming in ecstasy."

A tall white guy chimed in. "Brother, I didn't know black men ate pussy." I looked at him like he was crazy. "At two thirty we got a call about the screams. I knocked on the door, but when you didn't answer I opened it. I could see the young lady you were with spread-eagle on the dresser and you were eating like you were homeless. You eat better than a white boy." They all laughed.

An older woman began. "Young fella, you sure know how to make a woman feel special. I was in the adjoining room and watched you caress that young girl the whole night. I peeked in on you five times and if I wasn't sixty I would fuck you myself." Each person went on about them seeing me turn Tessa out.

One Spanish lady who spoke no English had her interpreter talk. "Boy, you tear a pussy up. What's your name?"

"My friends call me Mr. Roarke," I said proudly.

The manager caught up with me as I reached the elevators and handed me a bonus pass for a week's worth of free rooms. I thanked him and got onto the elevator.

Tessa didn't hear me enter the room; she was on the speakerphone with Mita and a few friends. Mita was asking what happened. "Give me all the juice."

Tessa started with how I set the mood. She told them about all the sucking and licking that I did. "Guess what else we did? I love it in my ass."

Suddenly a voice she didn't recognize said, "You let him put all ten inches in your ass?"

"Who else is on this phone? Which one of y'all knows that his dick is ten inches?"

Mita spoke up. "My cousin Tina, from uptown, is on the phone."

"You better start talking before I'm on my way to whip your ass," Tessa told Tina. Tina began to explain that she had met Roarke at Howard's homecoming last year. She thought he was a "Q" 'cause all the AKA's and Delta's were jocking him. "I took him back to my dorm and my roommate was being an ass and wouldn't leave. Roarke said he was fine with it if I was and dropped his pants. I realized he was at least ten inches because he kept hitting my diaphragm. It was just a one-night stand and I didn't even know his name until later."

Mita apologized. "Tessa girl, I didn't know."

Side note:

Fraternities and sororities, I have mad love for all of them, but they are not for everybody. I was from the hood so that's all I needed at that time of my life.

Back to the story:

After Tessa calmed down, she again began with the tale of our weekend together. She told them about the bag of chocolate kisses and how I retrieved them. "Girls, I was a chocolate pussy pie. The chocolate kisses were melting inside of me. As y'all know that's the hottest part of the body. So after an eternity he went all the way down to retrieve the kisses. By the time he licked my clit, which seemed like a lifetime, the kisses had melted and were running out of me. He picked me up, took me to the dresser, grabbed a pillow, and put it under my ass. He had me for breakfast, lunch, dinner, and dessert. I came over and over again until I fell asleep."

They all said "damn" together like a singing group.

I came up behind Tessa and she paused, about to tell the girls to hold on, but I shook my head and signaled her to continue. I pulled up her nightgown and began to eat her. Her voice started to get shaky and Mita was urging her to tell them more. Tessa stuttered and moaned and finally couldn't take anymore and screamed, "Yes!"

Mita and the other girls were yelling, "What's wrong, girl, why are you screaming?"

I bent Tessa over and started doing her doggy style. Now I was yelling, "Whose is it?"

And Tessa was saying, "Yours, Roarke, yours."

Mita yelled into the phone, "Y'all nasty," and hung up. We experimented all night with different positions and she fell back in exhaustion and went to sleep.

EGO:

I'm smiling from ear to ear for two reasons. One is that I am truly enjoying myself and two is that I planned for her girlfriends to hear, which is why I did it while she was on the phone. Now my reputation will become bigger than I can imagine because women talk and tell all their business. With those gossipy girlfriends of hers, not only will I have access to them, but it will lead to access to all their friends as well. You know the saying about you tell one friend and I will tell two friends and so on and so on? I might even become world-renowned. Everybody has some relatives and friends in the military and down South. Can you tell my head is bigger than this hotel?

Back to the story:

The weekend was over so I took her home and met her parents. When I saw her father, I recognized him from around the hood, but I didn't say anything. "So, you're Courtney, huh? It's a pleasure to meet you." Her mother extended her hand for me to shake.

Her father said, "Boy, that's not your name. I know you. Don't you know me?" I shook my head. "Yeah, you know me and they call you Mr. Roarke."

Of course I knew him, everybody on 7th and Kennedy worked for him. His street name was "Sugarman"; he sold cocaine. When the ladies went into the kitchen to get some drinks he said, "Son, I appreciate you acting like you don't know me, but it's okay, my wife and daughter know I have friends in the hood, but they don't know that I own that area." He told me that he would let me date Tessa on two conditions. "First, you can never tell Tessa or my wife what I really do for a living and second, if you ever think about hurting Tessa, I will kill you."

My heart jumped into my throat. "Kill me? Isn't that a little harsh?" Out of all the girls to fall in love with, I fall in love with the daughter of a drug kingpin.

At work on Monday, I had several messages from my boys and one from Sonya. Sonya was a lady that worked in my building that I used to date; she was also married. I went to her desk around noon but she wasn't there. I wanted to go out for lunch, so I headed toward the parking garage and there was Sonya, parked next to my car. "Get in," she said.

I told her no because she didn't have that type of control over me (anymore), but my dick was telling me "Get in, now!" I tried to reassure myself that I had Tessa and that was all I needed, so I got in my car and drove away blasting Chuck Brown.

Sonya:
Sonya was one girl that I shouldn't have dated; she was married. One of the women that worked with me hooked me up with her. She said she just wanted sex, no commitment. So I did her and ended up doing something that no playa should ever do: fall in love with some married pussy. Never ever fall in love with some pussy or dick that you can't have all the time. It will drive you crazy. Since she was married I used to

do her at lunchtime. Sonya was a small, dark-skinned girl, weighing about eighty-seven pounds, but that never stopped her. What she was lacking in height she made up in pussy. This was one of the deepest, wettest pussies I have ever had. *Deepwater I'm drowning.*

Since I knew I could put in work I thought I could tear this pussy up, so I caught myself taking it easy. She was little and I didn't want to hurt her. I put in about five inches and couldn't feel anything. I had to regroup and put in another three. She started smiling and said, "Is that it?" I put in the last two inches and she started fucking my brains out. She rode backward, frontward, and doggy style. Then she did this move I still use to this day.

She sat on top and told me to spin her, so I spun her around like a merry-go-round. At around the fourth spin her pussy spit out cum all over my dick, but she wanted more. This little girl was a real woman. She manhandled me for the next four hours. We did it everywhere I knew and all the ways that she knew. This girl was incredible; she amazed me over and over again.

As I said this little girl was big on pussy.

Vacean

Forever flowing,
Massive and complex,
Unknown to all for what is next.

Rushing in rapids,
Eternal soars,
Granales of millions to untouchable floors.

Back to the story:

That Friday, I went to Classics nightclub for happy hour. I loved free food, cheap drinks, and a busload of honeys. After a few drinks, my pager went off with an unfamiliar number. When I called, a young lady answered, but I didn't recognize the voice. "Did somebody page Roarke?" I asked.

"Yes, it's Simi Nita, I need a favor. I need a date for the Frankie Beverly concert tonight."

I said sure and got directions to her house and told her that I would pick her up shortly. I went home to shower, shave, and then was on my way. I loved me some Frankie Beverly and Maze.

We arrived at Constitution Hall around nine thirty. As we were walking up the stairs, I saw Mita at the front door taking tickets. She told me that she wanted to see me after we were seated, alone. I didn't like her thinking she had the upper hand so I said sure.

After seating Simi, I told her that I would go get some drinks and went back out to the lobby to find Mita. A security guard told me that Mita wanted to see me in the main office. I got directions from the guard and walked to the nearest elevator. I couldn't imagine what stunt this girl was trying to pull. I got off the elevator and smelled perfume in the hallway. I slowly opened the door to the office and she was sitting on the desk naked. She told me that if I didn't make her cum, she was going to tell Tessa that I was here with another girl.

When I looked down at her pussy, I saw that she had my initials cut into the hair. "Girl, you straight crazy, I'm outta here." She threatened me again, so what could I do? I turned back around and started playing with her clit and within minutes her juices started to flood the desk. I told her we were even and as I turned to leave she came up behind me and unzipped my pants. My dick popped out at attention and she started giving me head. I pushed her away and ran back to the elevator. I saw that my dick was all wet and sticking to my pants.

I went to the bathroom to clean up and then stopped by the bar to get Simi's Bacardi and coke. I ordered a double shot of gin for myself and went back to my seat. Simi asked if I was okay. "You look like you've seen a ghost." I told her I would be all right.

I was enjoying the opening act. Tommy Davidson was a local favorite and a good friend of mine. He was cracking me up and taking my mind off of what happened with Mita. While we were laughing she happened to slap my leg and noticed the wetness on my pants and then she saw my manhood. She began to stroke it gently. I pushed her hand off. "Are you not attracted to me?" I told her that I was but wanted to enjoy the concert for now.

The announcer came out. "Are you ready DC? Here they are Maze featuring Frankie Beverly."

Frankie came out in his trademark white baseball cap and linen outfit and started singing, *I Want to Thank You,* and then picked up the pace with *Southern Girl.* Everybody was on his or her feet dancing in the aisles. When he started singing, *Before I Let Go* I was in my own world, the Maze Zone. I felt a pair of hands gripping my ass. I really didn't want to look back, but I did and it was Simi. I turned her around and start riding her ass. I knew it was wrong, but I got caught up in the moment.

When Frankie sings, *Before I Let Go,* he goes into his trademark dance and starts saying, ah ah ah ah ah. There's one part of the song when he says, "There ain't no way that I can let you go before I know what to do with you 'cause you are my pretty baby, ah ah ah ah." The crowd goes wild when he does this. He stays on that note for about fifteen minutes.

Maze performed for three more hours. This was when you could go to a concert and the artist really put on a show for your money. Before Frankie left, he came back for an encore; even the security guards were dancing by now. Frankie finished with, "I love y'all, DC! Thank you!"

Maze

He knows what to do for us,
Called it intuition,
He talks about our joy and pain.

He appreciates the South,
With a tribute to southern girl,

He gives us the reason,
To love again.

He reminds us to not have affairs,
With the morning after.

Uplifts us constantly,
With his happy feelings,
Make it seem so simple,
When he talks about like magic.

Sets you up to go forward,
With before I let go,
During the course of time he shares,
How he hates being alone.

By his constant touring,
And live performances second to none,

He lets us know he still,
Loves us much too much.

After a kick-ass show, we left Constitution Hall with our clothes stuck to our bodies. We finally got to the car and as I opened her door she grabbed my neck and pulled me to her. "You don't want this booty?" She grabbed my belt and pulled me closer, my dick against her leg. She started kissing my neck and ears. I got weak and out of nowhere I heard Jodeci's, *Forever My Lady.* I pulled away from her and went around to the driver's side, got in, and pulled off. I put on Chuck Brown to clear my head and calm my nerves. They say music soothes the savage beast.

As I was driving, I glanced over at Simi and she had this strange look on her face. I asked if she was okay, but she didn't respond. Soon she started panting and moaning. I was thinking that this sista done lost her mind, but when I looked down I realized she was finger fucking herself. (Fellas, this is a beautiful sight when a woman can please herself. You don't bother her; just admire her work.)

I slowed down to watch her do her thing; I was loving this. I turned Chuck up and she was massaging her clit to the beat. She had one leg out of the window and the other on the dashboard. I was driving with my left hand and my right hand was in her pussy. All of a sudden I heard sirens. I pulled over and the officer asked for my license and registration. He asked how many drinks I had and gave me a sobriety test. When I passed he asked, "Why were you driving so slow?"

"Officer, you wouldn't believe it if I told you."

He said, "Young fella, try me." I told the officer to go to the passenger side door and take a look at my date pleasing herself. "What do you mean she's pleasing herself?" he asked.

what i do is
TABOO

He looked further into the car. Simi hadn't moved since we stopped. Her feet were still up and the lips of her pussy were shining in the moonlight. When the officer stood up he looked pleased. Knowing what he had just seen, I threw my trump card at him. "Am I free to go?"

"Young fella, you make sure you take care of that young lady. She looks like she needs some help, if you know what I mean." He smiled and patted me on the back. "You got your work cut out for you, I hope you can handle her." I got in the car, thanked the officer, and drove off.

I put my hand on her thigh and she said she wanted to go to a motel. My mind was telling me no, but my dick was saying, "Yes, hit it!"

I told her that I was involved with someone and that I should take her home. She got mad. "I don't give a fuck, you're mine tonight," and then she started to get loud and took a swing at me.

I tried to keep my cool. I calmed her down by telling her that I would pick her up tomorrow and take her to dinner. "Let's do it right, you're too fine to be at a motel. Motels are for hoes, I consider you a lady. Am I right?"

She said, "You're right, Roarke. I heard you were a real gentleman and you really are. Thank you for not taking advantage of me."

When I dropped her off at her house, I opened the car door, and walked her to the porch. We hugged and she apologized for her behavior and I told her that what happened tonight was between her and me.

I smiled as I walked to my car and I thought, *I don't believe she went for that lie; she done bumped her head. She won't see me again this year.* I was hungry after that episode, so I went to the Star Carryout in Southeast for some food.

Sandwich:

The Star has this submarine sandwich that is breakfast and lunch put together. It consists of steak, ham, egg, and cheese. The sandwich is so big Dre and I usually split one.

Back to the story:

I saw my boy Dre there. "What's up, Roarke?" We went inside and I ordered two sub sandwiches and began to tell Dre about my night at the concert and the ride home with Simi. All of a sudden I heard that Jodeci song, *I Can't Leave You Alone You Got Me Feening.* Dre asked, "What's wrong, you stopped talking."

"Never mind, man." Again I started to tell him what was happening and then Tessa appeared out of nowhere. She came over and kissed me on the cheek and then went to the counter to place her order. When I looked around I noticed this dude looking at me. "Dre, do you know that bama?"

"No, I thought you knew him. He's been staring at you since Tessa got here. I'm thinking this may be a stickup boy or something." Stickup boys were always lurking, especially this time of the morning.

When Tessa returned I told her about the guy standing by the wall. She started to laugh. "No he's not, he's with me." Then she walked over to him.

By now I was completely disturbed. I was trying to live right by denying myself all this new pussy and she was dating some bama. "Roarke, what are you going to do about that?"

I said, "Hey, they're just friends, you know I got friends too." I walked over. "What's up with y'all?"

The dude said, "I know you, they call you Roarke."

"Do I know you?" He mentioned Black and Curly from uptown; we went to school together. So I asked, "How do you know Tessa?"

what i do is
TABOO

He said, "We were friends from Suitland high school."

"Oh, so tell me some secrets about her."

He said there weren't any and Tessa started to laugh.

"What are you guys doing out at three o'clock in the morning?"

Dre came over and said, "Man, I hope you're not doing my boy Roarke's girl, 'cause I'll hurt you right here, right now." Then Dre started choking him. Tessa was screaming and hitting Dre on the back to make him stop. She said, "Tell your henchman to stop, you know he listens to you."

When the guy started gagging I told Dre to stop. Dre punched him a few times and then said you need to tell me what's up with you and Roarke's girl. The guy's nose started to bleed and he said that he and Tessa were just friends. The Chinese lady called our number. I gave her the number and grabbed Dre. I told Dre to meet me in the circle.

We ate on top of our cars and Dre said, "Why did you let that guy off that easy? I was ready to put him in the hospital." Dre was hardheaded; he always wanted to knock somebody out. Dre went into the trunk and grabbed a couple of beers. Just then Darnell, Reggie, and Kevin pull up.

I started to tell them about the night's events and Kevin, who knew Simi, said, "She always played hard to get with me." Then I told them about Mita threatening me and what happened in the office at Constitution Hall. The fellas were giving each other high-fives and were dying laughing about it. "Roarke, that's why I hang with you, people don't believe the shit that happens when we're together."

I said, "Thanks for validating me, Dre; folks just don't understand the power of the tongue."

The power of the tongue:

I can talk women into doing things they have never dreamed of. Along the way I had this woman that let me do her in the women's bathroom at work while everybody was at their desk. I don't know if I'm bold or just crazy.

Back to the story:

We sat there and shot the breeze until the sun came up. Everyone else left while Dre and I started to plot what we were going to do for the rest of the day; no time for sleep. Dre and I decided to meet at Sam's around ten o'clock that morning.

When I got home, I showered and ate breakfast. Dre called and told me that he was leaving. My pager was blowing up with numbers that I didn't recognize. I grabbed a bunch of quarters on the way out the door. When I got to Sam's, Dre was already talking to a honey, which meant I had to catch up. His pager went off, but he didn't recognize the number. I looked at his pager and noticed that it was the same number on mine.

Unknown phone numbers:

Never call phone numbers that you don't recognize from your home. Even though I did many young ladies in my basement, they never knew the house I lived in. I would pull in the alley, which was dark with barking dogs, open the basement door, and let them in. I would then go hide my car on the Maryland side so no one would know I was home. I didn't need any surprise visitors. After I broke them off properly, I would go out the front door and come back to the basement door and ride them around for ten minutes up some side streets and through other alleys so they wouldn't be able to return unless I brought them back. The things we playas do to keep where we live top secret.

what i do is
TABOO

Back to the story:

I went to the payphone to call the number and it was Paulette and her friend, these girls we met in Virginia. They invited us to a cookout in their neighborhood. I really didn't want to go, but Paulette told me it would be worth my time. I got directions and told them that we would be there.

On the way to the cookout Dre started to tell me that his girl, Andrea, usually pays him to be with her. I asked if Paulette would pay me too. He said, "I don't see why not."

When we picked up Andrea and Paulette, I asked them about the money and they said of course. "We'll give you each three hundred dollars just for the day."

I was excited. "Let's get this party started!"

Dre's girl actually looked better than mine. I didn't know how that happened, but he must have been driving that day. We had playa rules: whoever drove when we met honeys got the finest one. Most times I had the upper hand because I worked in an office full of women. There were only five guys in the whole building and there were 500 women. Remember, I said I loved my job.

Also, Dre and I never fought over girls because that was what happened in the movie *Cooley High*. That was why Cochise got killed 'cause him and Preach were fighting over a girl. That would never happen with Dre and me.

We pulled up to a large house on a hill; the driveway was about a mile long. I asked Paulette who lived here. "The twins, Camille and Carmen," she said.

The butler led us to the backyard; there was an Olympic size pool there, bigger than the one in the hood. Dre and I got a plate and sat down. We watched Paulette and Andrea work the party. The twins came over and introduced themselves. "Who are you with?"

Dre said, "We're with Paulette and Andrea."

The twins asked us to follow them to get drinks. I grabbed Dre's arm. "Come on, man." They took us to the pool house and told us to change into bathing suits. I dropped my shorts instantly.

Dre said, "Roarke, you trippin'. We don't know them like that."

Camille said, "I'll know him very well before he leaves today; *if* he leaves today."

They asked us our names. "I'm Roarke and this is my partner Dre."

Camille was very close to me and it was making me nervous. Carmen went over to Dre and told him to drop his shorts; he hesitated so Carmen grabbed him and started to unzip his shorts. I could see that he was thinking about something and he asked about the three hundred dollars that Andrea and Paulette were going to give us for the day. "Are y'all paying too?"

Carmen said, "Whatever Andrea and Paulette are paying you I will triple it."

Camille started to massage my manhood and Carmen finally got Dre's shorts off and was giving him head. While we were having these services performed in the pool house, I heard some noise and realized it was Andrea and Paulette. They came in and started to fight the twins. It was total chaos. I put my pants on, Dre pulled his back up, and we got the fuck out of there. I had the Maxima on two wheels hitting corners.

We finally arrived at Ollie's Trolley in Crystal City for some hamburgers and fries. Dre said, "Roarke, when I tell the fellas what happened today, you know they're going to say you're lying. The bad part about it is if I weren't there myself, I wouldn't believe it either. But crazy things happen when we're together."

I reminded Dre about M's cookout today. We got to the house about three o'clock that afternoon, and as we pulled

up, M yelled, "Dre, Roarke, park the car on the Maryland side so my guests can have somewhere to park." I saw some fellas on the block. I told them the cookout was going to start at six o'clock and they should bring ice and alcohol
cause we were going to party until Sunday night.

We filled the coolers with ice, beer, juice, lemonade, and iced tea. My brother got to the house first with his forty-ounce and a pack of Newport's. He still did the circles when he smoked. I gave love and said, "What's up?"

He said, "You know I had to be the first at this motherfucker. Hey M, where the deviled eggs at? I walked all the way down here and you ain't got any deviled eggs?"

She pulled up to him real close. "Boy, I will embarrass your ass and send you home if you don't stop that damn cussing. What do you think you're in the military on a ship or something?"

"Okay M, I'm sorry."

Dre shook his head. "Man, your brother is off the hook. He just says what he wants to anybody that's around."

"Yeah, that's why my mother always has to pull him up."

Two of my sisters arrived along with a few of my aunts and uncles. The DJ arrived and started setting up his equipment near the house. Around seven o'clock, three carloads of honeys arrived. I didn't know who they were so I asked my sister Faye. She told me that they were friends of hers, so when they came through the backyard I told the fellas that they were off limits because they were my sister's friends. We tried to stay away from each other's people. After a lot of debate, we all agreed that my sister's friends were off limits.

Pause:
I lied about not messing with each other's family members. I did Reggie's sister Darla. It was late one night and

around three o'clock one morning. I was coming home and I stopped at the Star to get a sandwich and she was there. We talked and laughed until our food was ready. She asked where I was going. I said back to my house. She asked if we could eat together. "You know, Reggie is out with one of them hoes and my mother doesn't come home until eight from the night shift at the hospital."

I told her, "No way, I will not get caught in that house."

She agreed and suggested we go to the basement. "You're playing with fire and you may get burnt."

She laughed. "Are you scared, Roarke? A nineteen year old scares you?"

I told her, "No, you don't scare me, but you know this isn't right. Meet me in the alley behind my house; just this once though." She lived across the street from my mother.

As we ate our food, we talked about everything from politics to current events. She got close and said, "Roarke, you are so smart, why do you have to be a dog? You would make a great husband."

I am well read if I do say so myself. I read any and everything, which allows me to operate in various circles. I have friends who are hustlers and friends that are politicians. I know people from the projects to the penthouse. My knowledge has supported me in many situations that have arisen.

After we ate she started to get frisky. I always let the woman be the aggressor and played hard to get; this turned them on. The more of a gentleman you acted like the more of a hoe they became. I guess it's the rejection as we all know rejection hurts, so the more I say no, the nastier they become until I have to serve them just what they want: my brick hard manhood pointing in their direction.

Now she was butterball naked saying, "I want it Roarke, for real, give it to me."

what i do is
TABOO

I say, "Look, before anything happens you have to swear that you will never tell Reg. You know I love him like a brother and you like a sister."

She said, "Okay, but does a sister do this?"

She started to...she started to...I can't believe this; she was bent over the sink in the basement near the washing machine hookup saying, "Put it in now, I swear I will keep it a secret."

So as I stuck the head in she hollered, "Yes," but instead of talking dirty to her, I made her promise with every pump that she would keep this a secret. I told her not even her girlfriends could know. "This is between you and me right?" She hollered, "I swear, Roarke. After you do me tonight I will let you have my summer paycheck." I was shoving harder and harder. I knew that I had arrived; she was going to give me her paycheck.

I put in another forty-five minutes of work until she couldn't stand it anymore and collapsed onto the floor. I put a sleeping bag under her and lay on the floor beside her. She asked how I lasted so long. The guys at Morgan State where she went to school couldn't last more than ten minutes.

I told her, "It is totally in the mind. I can't cum until you do. It's my trademark."

She laughed and said, "So that's why the girls come out of the alley limping in the early hours of the morning."

"It's my job to make you happy," I said.

Now I tell her that I want her to still be my friend even though we have crossed the line.

In the morning I tried to put it back in at least five times, but she kept saying she was sore. She said, "I'm not used to that much penetration, can I come over tomorrow?" I told her, "Wrong answer. You know you can't be seen over here." She thought about it and finally agreed to just put the head in, but when I did she scooted backward and it was halfway in her. I started to move forward and then it was all the way in. I grabbed her waist and started to work her in a circular motion, which hit everything from the clit to the butt hole, so all her senses could be massaged. This drove her crazy and she loved it. About twenty minutes later I stopped because she had three different orgasms.

Yes, I said three different types of orgasms; she had a vaginal, a clitoral, and a multi-orgasm. I know my orgasms, do you?

Side Note:

Fellas, to keep a woman happy in bed you must not cum until she is totally fulfilled, and she must reach her peak before you. Your job is to do everything to accomplish this mission. Sucking, licking, and eating for hours if you have to: she must be smiling before she leaves your bed.

Back to the story:

DJ Slim was pumping the music as more people arrived. My sister, Regina, was at the spades table with her husband beating all the takers. Everybody was having a good time. I asked M if she needed anything else for the party. "Yes, I need you to go enjoy yourself and get this party started," she said.

So, Reg, Dre, and I go get plates while Darnell, Mitch, and Tyrone got the drinks. We found a corner to stand in to eat our food and watched the honeys. Before I started drinking I got another plate. I needed to be full before I started drinking so I could keep my composure. There was nothing like a drunk at a lawn party acting like a fool.

I finished my plate and my beer and told the fellas, "Let the party begin." DJ Slim was cranking, but nobody was dancing. We walked across the yard and grabbed three regular looking honeys from the neighborhood and started dancing with them. Once we started dancing, other people started too. The girl I was dancing with turned around for me to ride her ass. I realized it was a nice ass, if I did say so myself. It was actually *perfect*.

Perfect ass:

A perfect ass is an ass that's not too big and not too small. It's curved perfectly under the cheeks for palming, not up too high on the back, and not too low on the back of the knees. A perfect ass is the size of a volleyball.

Perfect Ass

All through history it has amazed us,
Some cultures want more of this,
Some cultures buy more of it,
A few cultures were born with it.

Men watch in awe,
Women watch in admiration.

They have been described in many songs.

At one time one culture didn't realize its beauty,
And other cultures just envied.

But either you have it or you don't.

Side note:

To have other girls recognize you, go do something with an average looking girl. Women recognize a man when he is with someone else. It goes back to they want what someone else already has. So women or men, when you see a regular looking guy or girl with someone fine, it makes her step up her game to do better because she now adores you and wants you. So ladies and fellas, just chill 'cause the fine one that you really want is coming soon to get you.

Back to the story:

Tessa, Mita, Priscilla, Angel, and Roxanne arrived around eight o'clock, but I played it off like I didn't see them. Never let them see you sweat. While I was dancing I saw Tessa talking to M and after the song I walked over. I gave her a peck on the cheek and she leaned over and kissed me on the lips. "I seen you nasty boy. Did you enjoy her ass better than mine?"

My mother walked away. "You know I was just dancing." She said, "Roarke, don't make me cut you."

I said, "Stop playing, girl, I don't take threats very well." She said, "Don't play with me, Roarke."

Pause:

I really don't take threats well at all. An unnamed girlfriend threatened me back in the day with a knife. I bent her thumb back so far I broke it. So please don't threaten me.

Back to the story:

I asked Tessa if she had gotten some of M's potato salad yet. She shook her head and I told her to wait while I got her a plate. At the buffet table, someone squeezed my butt. I didn't want to turn around because I knew it was going to be trouble. I just walked away from the table, but I could hear footsteps behind me. I slowed down and as I turned the plate of food went flying out of my hand; it was Mita. "What's up, Roarke, did you enjoy the other night?"

I played stupid. "I don't know what you're talking about, girl, you crazy." I felt like punching her in the face. I don't advocate violence against women, but sometimes, ladies, y'all will push a brotha to snap.

Mita started getting loud. "You know you want this pussy. It's better than T's tight pussy."

I started to walk away when I saw my boys coming to my rescue. Dre grabbed Mita by the arm. "Be gone, girl, before you get hurt." She swung on Dre, but Reg grabbed Mita and pulled her away fast. I had to grab Dre because he would've choked her. I asked the fellas to keep her away while I got T out of there.

Once I found T I told her we needed to leave. She asked, "Where's my potato salad?" I told her that M would make her a special batch of potato salad, but right now we had to go. The heels she had on were slowing us down so I put her on my back and carried her to my car. Once in the car, I was thinking of some discount places to take her. My money was funny so I had to think of what I could do with a hundred dollars. We needed food, hotel accommodations, and some fun.

We went to Georgetown to window shop, then to a restaurant by the waterfront. I ordered drinks and dessert and then we were off to the T-house where I made sweet love to her. I brought out her adventurous side here. Tessa didn't know what a T-house was. She said since she was where sluts lay she would act like one. The loving was so good in the T-house I felt that I was with more than one woman. She was inventing all these new sounds and positions. Get yourself a tall girl, that's all I can say.

T-house:

T-house is short for tourist home. They are in most neighborhoods and you pay by the hour. The fellas call them fuck shacks. When your money is funny or you just have a real freak, you go to the T-house.

Back to the story:

As we left the T-house, Tessa asked, "How do you know so much about what a woman needs?"

I told her that I read all types of books: romance novels to magazines and I talk to women. "I try to do what other men don't do; wine and dine. I don't want to just fuck you; I want to make love to you. I like to tease the mind, body, and soul, have you always wanting more." My biggest turn on is an educated woman. Education does not mean she has three or four college degrees. It means she has knowledge and knows how to use it to her advantage, that's real education.

Speaking of surprise she says, "How was the show?"

We started laughing. I said, "If I tell you what happened that night you'll be mad."

She said, "Try me, I can handle it."

"Okay, here it is. I told the fellas and they freaked out."

"Before you go any further," she said, "I already know what Mita did." My mouth dropped to the floor. "I sent her to try you and she told me you ran out of there like the police was after you."

"Hold up." I was in shock. "You sent her there? What type of freak are you?" Now I was pissed. I rode down the street like Mad Max. She tried to explain and asked me to slow down.

I pulled over. "This better be good."

"Mita is to me what Dre is to you. She protects me from harm."

I smiled. "But what harm could I be to you?"

Tessa said that the last man that she was with broke her heart, but he's no longer here to tell anyone.

I said, "Hold up, did your father have anything to do with that?"

She looked out of the window. "Let's just say it got handled."

I'm feeling kind of shaky now; her father must have killed the last dude. "I plan to be faithful to you, but you know that sometimes things happen that you can't control."

Tessa took my hand in hers. "Roarke, talk to me."

"T, maybe you're not the women I thought you were."

"Come on now, Roarke, this is what you do with your boys, protect each other, lie for one another, and sometimes kill for each other. It's a crime that I know how to play the game, but remember who my father is, he invented the game."

"You got a point there, but I'm going to have to watch you, T."

After our conversation ended, I resumed driving. "Roarke, I think we like each other because we are so much alike and that scares me. I didn't know what you would do to me after putting Mita on you."

"T, you really don't know me do you? I am not the vengeful type. I don't like what you did, but I guess I deserved it. But from now on let's be straight with each other. Hold up, how did you know I was going to the show?"

"I know people too, Roarke. I don't know Simi personally, but I have friends that know her, so they hooked this up for me. So what did Simi do?"

"After the concert, on the way to her house, she masturbated in the front seat and then flicked off when I wouldn't take her to a motel."

Tessa said, "That was not part of the plan."

"Well, now it's my turn to ask you some questions and I need the truth; who was that bama that Dre beat up in the carryout the other night?"

Tessa said that he was an old classmate from high school. "He asked me to go to the show with him long before I met you."

"And how did he know my folks from uptown?"

She replied that he had cousins who lived uptown. Now that I got that out of her, I felt better about her, but I didn't trust her anymore. But who am I not to trust someone, the man that will do your cousin, your momma, your sister, and your girlfriend. She shouldn't believe me and I shouldn't believe her. When we got to her house, I walked her to the door, kissed her cheek, and was grateful that the night was finally over.

Pause:

This is a public service announcement. Never, ever date someone that's smarter than you. Let me break that down. Someone that's smarter than you already knows which moves you're going to make before you make them. They know what you're thinking. You think you're two steps in front of them and actually they are fifty steps in front of you.

Example:

Years ago there was a couple where the man was cheating on the wife, and he thought he was a playa. So by him not being smarter than her, this is what happened. He was out at a gentleman's club (AKA strip club). He had plans to bring two strippers to a T-house when they got off work. I told y'all he was a playa. So it was about two in the morning and he and the strippers were leaving the club. As they walked the entire parking lot, he couldn't find his car and thought someone had stolen it. He didn't realize that his wife had been there took the car and sold it.

The next day he came home from work and his wife asked him where the car was so she could run some errands. He lied for the next two years claiming it was in the repair shop.

what i do is
TABOO

As I said, his wife was fifty steps in front of him. Take my advice and stay away from mates that are smarter than you. This is a sad but true story.

Back to the story:

It was Sunday morning, but I wasn't one who went to church. Yes, I believe in God, but in my mind I'll hook up with Him when I'm older, around forty or fifty. But on this particular Sunday, two good friends, Penny and Rita, asked me to go to church with them and I agreed not knowing that I wouldn't be out of there until three o'clock in the afternoon. Penny and Rita had a bet that I would pull out and not go, but I fooled them. When they pulled up I was waiting on the front porch.

Pause:

Penny and Rita were like my conscience. (Let your conscience be your guide.) *I Know What You're Saying, Know What You're Doing, Know What You're Planning.* That's a song from the late 70s.

Back to the story:

The temple was ten minutes from my house, but we were late so we had to sit in the balcony. The church was packed and we couldn't find seats together. The choir was singing about the goodness of Jesus and had the church hollering and screaming. I hadn't been to church in a while so I felt like a fish out of water. Then came Reverend Willie Wilson, pastor of the temple. The man was respected in the hood for what he stood for and he was a world-renowned pastor. The pastor began the sermon with the meaning of manhood. I felt that he was speaking directly to me. He said, "A man needs to be a real man and stop describing his manhood by what's below his belt." I felt so good after hearing this message. I was thinking, *This man was on fire for the Lord and I was a piece of crap.* We went to IHOP on Branch Avenue after church and talked about the sermon.

Penny asked if I liked the service. I told her I thought Reverend Wilson was talking to me. "I know I'm a hoe and have been living foolishly for years now."

Rita said, "So what are you going to do about it?"

I told them about Tessa. "I think I love her, she's the one."

They were so excited for me. "We're so proud of you, please tell us more about her."

As I told them about the warm and fuzzy feelings that I got being with Tessa tears started running down my face.

Penny hugged me. "Roarke, you for real this time."

I told them that I had never felt this way before and every time I was about to do something that I had no business doing, I would hear a Jodeci song and I would stop dead in my tracks.

I told them about the dinner at Chesapeake and Rita was shocked. "She met your mother? What does your mother think about her? Because you never let women meet your mother. It was years before you let us meet her."

"M liked her and invited her to the cookout."

Penny asked, "What do you plan to do with her since you think you're in love?"

I told her that this was a really delicate situation and I really didn't know what to do. I reminded them that the last time I was in love, I was sixteen and she broke my heart. "That's why I'm the man I am today."

"Okay," Rita said, "when do we get to meet the woman that has got you all shook-up? She must be one hell of a woman if she has changed the way you think about women."

what i do is
TABOO

Another Forgotten Lover

It's daylight, I don't want
To turn over.

Who could she be?
Did she enjoy it?

Me, just another notch
On the bedpost.

Why do I put myself through this?
Why do I treat women like this?
I actually love them,

My mother was a good lady,
My sisters are good women,
Where did I get this pattern from?
Am I sick or just a sex fanatic?

Now I remember, my first love
Broke my heart
Now that's all I do.

So looks like there's
Another forgotten lover.

As the waitress brought our food, I looked over my shoulder and saw Dre, Reg, Darnell, and Mitch with about ten women. My eyes were about to pop out of my head because all these women were fine. I asked myself, *Where did they find these fine women?* Every now and then the fellas got lucky, but ten at one time, I was impressed.

They came over to the table and I introduced Dre and the fellas to Penny and Rita. Reg said, "Roarke, where'd you get those from? They're cute."

"Reg, it's not like that, we went to church this morning."

Everybody started laughing. "You at church, Roarke?"

As they walked away I grabbed Mitch's arm. "Where y'all get those honeys from?"

He laughed. "At M's cookout. Remember you left early?"

I was standing there with my mouth wide open. As I sat back down, I heard that Jodeci song, *Forever My Lady.*

I told Penny and Rita about the song and they were all smiles. "Lil brother, you got it bad and that ain't good."

We left the place and drove out of the parking lot and that's when I saw Mita and Simi sitting in a car. I started thinking about Tessa and my conversation with her about the way she handled things. She had me blind now; I thought I had the ability to convince people to do anything; I guess she had the same power.

We got back to my house and I told the girls that I wanted them to meet Tessa soon. "I'll set something up this week."

M came out onto the porch and the girls went up and hugged her. She asked, "What you got my boy doing this early in the morning, on a Sunday no less?" Penny told M they took me to church. "To church, girls, bless your heart," M shouted. "You two ladies are going to heaven; you brought my boy to church. Can I pay you?" My mother loved these girls because they kept me out of trouble. M made small talk asking the girls what they had been up to. Rita told her that she was about to graduate from Howard University and that Penny had graduated in May. M gave them each a twenty-dollar bill and told them to treat themselves to something nice. "When I hit the lottery come by and see me 'cause that's when I can really pay you for opening his eyes."

I said, "Come on M, my eyes aren't closed, I just needed a little push."

Penny said, "More like a shove." Now everyone was laughing.

My pager went off and I excused myself. The number wasn't familiar so I hesitated as I dialed from home. On the third ring a female answered. "Hi sweetie."

I didn't recognize the voice. "Excuse me, did you page me?"

She answered, "Yes, it's me, Tessa. Roarke, you still don't know my voice?"

I played it off. "I was just playing with you. Where are you?" She said that she was around the corner from me and asked if I was at home. I said, "Come over here. I want you to meet some people.

She pulled up about ten minutes later with Essence cranking and the top down on her car. She came up to the porch, greeted my mother, and was introduced to Penny and Rita as my fiancée. I ran out of the house just then. Penny and Rita were checking her out now. Rita circled her as Penny stared her up and down. Penny started with the questions first. "You got gold or something on your booty, 'cause you sure got Roarke hooked."

T blushed. "He's the one with the gold down there. I love him."

M started to well up. "You love him?"

Then it was Rita's turn. "Where do you live? You got kids? Where do you work? Do you go to Howard University? Why do you think you're good enough for Roarke?"

After answering the barrage of questions they all seemed satisfied and happy and ended the conversation with a hug. M stated that she had to go to the supermarket, which was an all day trip, Rita said she had a date, and Tessa was on her way to meet the girls and said that she would stop by later. Penny and I were left alone so we went to the basement to watch the game. She was a big basketball fan and it was the playoffs. The Lakers were beating the Pistons senseless; Magic Johnson was showing off.

I was playing darts while she was watching the game. During halftime Penny challenged me to a game of darts. I suggested we bet on each dart. "All right, how about a dollar a dart?"

I said, "Too low."

"Okay, five dollars a dart."

I told her that was still too low.

"Well, name your price?"

I said, "Clothes. These are the rules: whoever is the farthest away from the bull's-eye has to take something off."

Penny agreed. "You know I'm good at this game, so I'll go first."

I threw my dart and missed the whole board. She threw her dart and hit the third circle. Since we already had our shoes off, I took off my shirt. The next round she went first and hit the third circle again. Now it was my turn and I hit the bull's-eye, so she had to take off her stockings. About fifteen minutes into the game we were standing in the middle of the basement naked, staring at each other. Penny pulled her skirt back on and reached for her bra, but I stopped her and touched her nipples. She pushed me away and said, "They're tender."

"Well, can I lick one?" Penny kept saying no, but didn't stop me from getting her onto the bed. "You have a beautiful body, let's just make each other cum."

She said, "Say what?"

I told her again. "And no penetration." She agreed. I began sucking her nipples, as we positioned ourselves in a 69 position. Then I had a better idea, I tried one of my trademark moves: the 1069; it's a thousand times better than 69.

what i do is
TABOO

I know you're curious about what this move is. Get out your pen, paper, and camera.

I laid Penny on her stomach with her head pointing toward the bottom of the bed. I lay on her back slightly so I wouldn't crush her and put my head at her ass. Her head was slightly tilted by my dick. As I licked her asshole I had a clear view of her clit. As I was licking her asshole and clit, she was licking my balls, dick, and asshole. As it got more intense I was licking the walls of her pussy. She had at least six orgasms. We were sweating and sighing after those world-class orgasms. Then I heard a knock on the basement door.

We scrambled to put our clothes back on and Penny dashed upstairs. After about ten minutes I opened the door, it was Tessa. "Were you sleeping?"

I told her, "Yes, after last night and waking up early this morning for church, I was tired. Excuse my basement, I really need to clean."

We talked for a while before she remembered. "I have some errands to run for my mother. I can call you later or you can call me."

She tried to kiss me, but I put my hand over my mouth. "Girl, I got morning breath, it don't taste good." I couldn't have her kiss me with my mouth smelling like Penny's booty, which was mighty tasty. "Uh, thanks for looking out."

Then I said, "That's what love will make you do." Now I felt bad for lying on a Sunday.

Penny waited until Tessa's car was out of sight before she returned to the basement. I asked if she was okay and she replied, "Yes," and laughed. I told her we needed to talk and gestured to the couch. She said, "Yes, but me first. I had the most powerful orgasm. While you and T were talking I was upstairs at the dining room table pleasuring myself with a banana." I was at a loss for words and tried to figure out how

I could salvage this friendship. Then before I could begin she asked, "Roarke, can you cum for me?"

"Come on, Penny, we need to stop. As much fun as I just had you know we need to stop. What if I tell Rita?"

Penny started laughing hysterically. "This is why Rita won't be alone with you, she has always wanted you."

"Stop playing, Penny."

She wasn't joking. "For real, Roarke. Haven't you noticed every time you call her to hang out she brings me? I've known for about two years and I kept her secret. But the secret that you didn't know was that I wanted you, too."

Side note:

Ladies, never tell your girlfriends what you don't do sexually with your man. If you do you are basically giving him to your girlfriend. Because what you don't do she does and is an expert at it. So be complete, women. Suck it; fuck him, pussy and ass, and hundreds of positions 'cause good pussy will make a man stay, sometimes forever.

Back to the story:

I walked Penny to the door, knowing that this had to end. When I opened the front door my boy Dre was walking up to the house. Dre always rescued me. "What's up, Roarke, hey Penny, what's up for the day?"

I said, "I'm with you, Dre, anything you want to do."

Dre said, "Let's roll." I hugged Penny and told her that we would talk later.

Ten minutes later I was on the road with Dre. He kept looking at me and finally asked, "Roarke, you got that look on your face. What happened today?"

"I hate to say it but you're not going to believe this."

"Roarke, you know I believe everything you say, 'cause most of the times I'm with you."

what i do is
TABOO

I told Dre about the basement scene with Penny. "I think it's time to hang up my playa card, retire my basement, and burn my black book. I'm tired of living like this. Even though we had a lot of fun, I want to settle down with Tessa; I really think she's the one."

We pulled into Anacostia Park and Dre said, "Congratulations man; you've found a real woman. Do you want to marry her or what?"

"I don't know, Dre. I think I need to come clean with her and let her know who I really am." Dre reminded me not to tell her everything; some things should stay in the vault.

Soon we saw Reg and Darnell pull up and I updated them on the situation with Tessa. There was silence, then laughter. "Burn your black book!" Darnell laughed.

Reg said he wanted the black book. "You've had some freaks." When I tell the fellas that I was thinking about marriage, Dre said, "If this is the one, we're going to give you a bachelor party that will go down in history; we're talking Guinness Book of World Records."

I called Tessa and left a message telling her that I had something really important that we needed to discuss. About thirty minutes later, she called and I told her that I would meet her at her house in fifteen minutes. I was really nervous, but I felt that this was the right person for me and it felt like the right time.

When I got to the house, I was shaking so badly that I tripped and fell. Now I was on the ground laughing and tears were running down my face. Tessa and her parents ran out of the house.

"Are you all right?" Her father helped me up and her mother wiped my face. I told them that I was fine and we walked into the house. Now they were really curious to know what was going on.

"This is really hard for me," I started.

Her father jumped up. "Boy, if you're going to say something to hurt my daughter, I'm going to kill you before you say it."

Mrs. Williams said, "Sit down and let the boy speak."

I began again. "This has been hard because it makes me uncomfortable to say these words, but it makes me feel very happy inside. Mr. and Mrs. Williams, I would like to marry your daughter." Tessa started to cry and her parents looked dumbfounded. "I really love Tessa and I know she is the one." Her mother asked if I was sure. "Yes madam, in a year I would like to set a date and marry Tessa." I got down on one knee with T's hand in mine; she was balling now. "T, I don't have a ring right now, but I really love you."

She started shaking and blurted out, "Yes Roarke, yes. I will marry you." I stood up and we hugged.

Mr. Williams shook my hand. "Boy, I knew I liked you for my baby girl from the start."

"Do you approve, Mr. Williams?"

He replied, "Yes, and as long as you're good to her I'll be happy."

When I got home I told M and she sat me down for a talk. "I think you made a good choice, but let me warn you. This year is going to be your toughest year to resist temptation. Everybody, including your best friends, is going to put up roadblocks and create havoc. It's going to be a year of total chaos." I told M that she was always trying to scare me. "Boy, mark my words." Of course I didn't listen.

Mothers:

For some reason God gave mothers the intuition to see into the future. My mother knows everything. Whatever she said since I was a child has happened. Good and bad. So listen to your mother, she knows.

what i do is
TABOO

Rojena (my mother)

Started with nothing,
Ended with everything,
Taught so many,
Healed many wounds.

Soothed many souls.

Very caring and giving,
What a rare find,
Often chastised you,
But with a loving heart.

Always wanted more for you,
Than you wanted for yourself,
Won't hurt a soul,
Unless you mess with her kids.

Still teaching,
Even though she's no longer here.

Back to the story:
 Sunday at church, Reverend Wilson was on fire and I felt good. I even got my brother, Ronald, to go with me. His nickname is "Shake" because as a child he would dance like he was shaking something. While we were listening to the reverend, Shake bumped me. "Roarke, look at that honey right there."
 "No Shake, I'm trying to get some Word here."
 "Come on," he said, "one second."
 I glanced over and yes she was the bomb. I whispered, "Leave me alone."

He started laughing. "Since you're getting married you think you're better than me?"

"Shake, I am not having this conversation with you in church."

He let it drop, but as we were leaving church, he was pulling me again. "Roarke, look at that." I put my hand over his mouth and tried to move him out the door as quickly as possible. Once we get outside he was hollerin' at every woman in the parking lot. His favorite line was, "Come here, shorty, have you ever had a taste of a milkshake? I'll shake you up." I thought it was a whack line, but some women loved themselves some Shake. My brother has seven children by six different women, so I guess he's doing something right.

Shake wanted to go to the liquor store before I took him home, so we stopped on MLK. He got beer and some cigarettes and I got some chips. As we were leaving the store this honey asked me where they could get wine coolers? "In this store right here." Her girlfriend went into the store and she came around the car to talk to me.

"What's your name?" she asked.

I finally stuttered, "Roarke."

She told me her name was Tiffany. Her face was okay, but her body was amazing. She was wearing a halter-top and mini–skirt. Her nipples were like bullets and she had real thick legs. She asked what I had planned for the rest of the day. I told her that I would drop off my brother and then later I was meeting some friends for dinner at the Waterfront. She asked for my pager number.

"Why would you want that?" I asked.

My brother jumped in the conversation and gave her the number. Her girlfriend returned to the car and Tiffany yelled, "I'll page you later tonight."

I started yelling at Shake. "Why'd you do that, you know I'm getting married."

what i do is
TABOO

He turned and gave me this look. "Man, I don't care, as thick as that youngin' was, I'll do her for you. When she pages you give her my number, you know I'll shake her up." He did his shake move to make sure I knew what he was talking about.

We cruised the streets taking the long way back to his house. As we got near Eastover Shopping Center, my pager went off. I found a payphone and a girl answered. "Hey Roarke, this is Tiff."

I was like, "Who?"

She said, "Tiff, I met you two hours ago at the Chinese store."

"Oh, hey, now I remember you, what's up?"

She asked if I was still going to dinner with my friends and I said, "Yes, is there something better for me to do?"

She waited a moment and then replied, "You can explore some new pussy today."

I dropped the phone and just stood there.

Shake got out of the car and came over to me. "You okay, Roarke? What did that freak say?"

I got back on the phone and asked her to repeat what she said so Shake could hear. His eyes grew wide. "Hook me up, Roarke; let me get at that youngin'."

I told her my plans couldn't be changed, but that I appreciated the offer. Now I got another crazy girl on my hands. She started yelling, "Are you turning me down?"

I told her it wasn't like that. "I already have someone special." This did not help.

"So what's having a girlfriend got to do with you getting some new pussy?" I apologized for calling and that just made the situation worse. "I knew you couldn't handle this pussy anyway. I need a real man to attack this pussy, not a wimp like you." I hung up the phone and thought, *Who does she think she is, doubting my manhood?* Now I was mad and blaming

Shake. If he hadn't given that freak my pager number I wouldn't have to deal with this situation. I dropped Shake off and was on my way home to relax.

As I passed 23rd Street, I saw the fellas sitting at the powerhouse, so I stopped and sat with them for a while.

Bobbie was there. I hadn't seen him in a while and he asked, "Roarke, I hear you getting married, do I know her?"

I told him that I didn't think so. "I met her when you were locked up." I left after a few minutes and went on home.

M heard me come in and came downstairs to talk to me. I love my mother. She knew what I needed and when I needed it and I really needed her ear now. I told her about my day starting with church. "Reverend was off the hook and even Shake enjoyed the sermon." She had a good laugh and then I told her about Tessa. "Ever since I told Tessa that I wanted to marry her, all hell has broken loose." I told her about Tiffany.

"Baby, it will only get worse. I told you, this is only the beginning. I pray that you are strong enough to handle it." I told M I was praying for the same thing. She asked, "Are you still going to dinner later?"

"Yes," I replied and she told me to enjoy myself.

"I'll talk to you tomorrow, I have plans of my own tonight."

"See you, love you."

"I love you, too," she said and left.

I decided to take a nap since I wasn't leaving until six o'clock. I took off my church clothes and fell into a deep trance. I dreamed about old girlfriends, my first one from the second grade, to all the others from uptown, southeast, southwest, northeast Baltimore, Virginia, even the New York girls were chasing me.

One girl had a pair of pliers in her hand and the others had sticks, whips, and bricks. I'm running for my life and they're smiling and singing, "Mr. Roarke, make our fantasies come true."

I'm crying like a punk because they caught me. The girl with the pliers starts to move toward my balls. She grabs them and I'm yelling, "Stop bitch." She smiles as she grips them harder and my balls feel like they're going to explode. I wake up sweating and breathing hard. I was so frightened by this dream that I couldn't close my eyes.

I woke up and took a shower. That seemed to help clear my head. I put on a black suit and a nice silk tie. The dinner wasn't just any dinner, but a business meeting; I was in the process of opening a consulting firm. I had to give an informal presentation of services that I was going to offer to a Mike Phillips, the CEO of Simms, Inc. and a few of his colleagues.

I arrived at the restaurant twenty minutes early to ensure that everything would go as planned. I ordered food and drinks and waited for the meeting to begin. Once underway the presentation was a success, the executives were pleased with my ideas and skills. As we were rapping up, they noticed a table of young ladies sitting across from us. Mr. Phillips was eyeing one lady in particular, but she wasn't paying any attention to him. I suggested that if I could get him a date with the young lady that he would be my first client. He agreed and we shook on it.

I went to the table and asked the ladies if they would like another round of drinks. They agreed and I went to the bar to make the order. I then went back to the table and struck up a conversation. I told them about my friend Mike. "He sent the drinks and wanted to know if he could have a date with you." I pointed to the light-skinned sister across the table from me.

The spokeswoman for the group replied, "What's in it for my girlfriend? Can one or all of us have you?"

"Hey," I said, "the alcohol must be potent tonight. I just wanted her to go out on a date with him."

Again the spokeswoman replied, "Yes, I heard you but what are you willing to give up?"

I told them that I was trying to start a new business and at the moment I wasn't in a position to offer much, but was willing to discuss it further if the young woman agreed to the date with my client. So I gave the spokeswoman my pager number and she put the name and number of the young lady on a napkin.

When I got back to the table, I gave Mike the number. He pulled a contract out of his briefcase and we both signed. I was in the mood to celebrate so I ordered a Blue Hawaiian. My pager went off just then and I excused myself. On the way to the payphones my pager went off again, twice this time. But these were all unfamiliar numbers. The first page was from Mita, which was a short conversation; she didn't want nothing but trouble. The next page was Melissa and after a little small talk I told her that I was busy and would talk to her later. The last call was from Tiffany and it really freaked me out because the number on my pager was almost the same as the number I was calling from on the payphone. Tiffany asked, "Will I see you tonight?" I paused and told her that I would call her back. She gave me her pager number and I hung up and returned to the table.

As I got closer to my table, I noticed that there was a woman there. I introduced myself and the woman turned around. "Hi, Roarke." It was Tiffany.

The gentlemen at the table asked, "Do you two know each other?"

"Yes," she replied. "Roarke and I go way back. We're actually meeting later tonight to discuss some future business, right Roarke?"

I had to agree. I didn't want her to blow this deal for me, but she could see the steam coming from my ears. I couldn't

what i do is
TABOO

believe this girl was trying to play me. She obviously didn't know whom she was messing with.

We made small talk at the table and soon the check arrived. Mr. Phillips paid and left the waiter a $200 tip; he almost fainted when they told him to keep the change.

Tiffany asked me to stay at the table for a few minutes to go over some details for our meeting. I walked my business associates to the door and returned to the table to put this girl in her place.

When I returned to the table it was cleared and set for two with a small candle and flower in the center. As I sat down, Tiffany blew out the candle. "I just wanted us to get a little closer." I'm about to tell her off when I realized her top was down and her breasts were on the table; they were gorgeous. Her nipples were like bullets and I had to touch them. Then she said, "I'm yours." I heard that Jodeci song in my head again. I felt dizzy. *Forever My Lady, It's Like a Dream.*

"Do you live near here?" I asked.

"I have an apartment at the Marbury Plaza on Good Hope Road."

I said, "Let's go to your place." She smiled, fixed her top, and we were off to the parking garage. I opened the passenger door for her, but she opened the back door and pulled me into the car on top of her. Her skirt was up and her top was down. Passionately we kissed. I was enjoying myself too much to think about getting up.

Eventually I got into the driver's seat, leaving her in the backseat. Man, did she put on a good show. I pulled up to Marbury Plaza and parked while she put her clothes on. I knew I needed to get away from her but I couldn't.

We took the elevator and she pressed the button for the sixth floor. The elevator went up about two floors, stopped, and then the lights went out. At first, I was terrified, but then

I felt hands all over me, rubbing and grabbing. It was incredible. What more erotic place to do the nasty than the elevator? I couldn't have planned it better, but not with her. I was trying to avoid her in this small elevator, but she was attacking me like a Doberman on a poodle. She pulled me to the floor and pinned me there. She pulled my zipper down and began to deep throat my manhood. I shouted for her to stop, but she replied, "You're mine tonight. All mine and you are going to explore this pussy and enjoy the hell out of it."

I finally got to my feet and began backing away toward the light beneath the door. All of a sudden she was on me again. I laid there in silence. If I knew what was next, I would have pried the elevator door open with my teeth. She just sat down on my manhood and rode me like I was a horse at the Kentucky Derby.

Just then the lights in the elevator flickered and I heard the motor begin, so I jumped up, pulled up my pants, and hit the next button. Once the doors opened I ran down the stairwell as if I had robbed a bank. After I got to the car and calmed down I heard a love song dedication on the radio. It was Tessa dedicating an LTD song to me. *We Both Deserve Each Other* by Jeffrey Osbourne played, as tears rolled down my face. I wondered how and why I put myself in these situations.

When I got home I noticed people outside, but as I reached my front door a horn blew. I walked toward the car and the rear window came down revealing a group of girls. I walked back to the house when I heard, "I haven't forgotten what you and Dre did to me, Roarke." I tried to get a good look at the girl, but as I got closer to the car they drove away.

I didn't have any idea what turned a person evil, but I had a hand in this one. The girl that was in the car was an old girlfriend; the only ex-girlfriend that I wasn't on good terms with. Her name was Kathleen Frazier, but she called herself

Kat girl and she was a true hood rat. My mother warned me about trying to convert a hood rat into a lady, but I didn't listen. I tried to show her the nicer things in life: took her to shows and the theater and nice shopping malls and Georgetown. I took her to places she never knew existed and tried to show her the world outside of the hood. But after all that, she claimed that I didn't treat her right.

Kat and I became friends and occasionally we would hang out, but she always wanted Dre to come. I think she liked Dre more than me, but Dre and I had a code: never let a woman come between us. Well, the beginning of the end of our relationship began one morning when Kat called to say that she wanted to treat Dre and me to Chesapeake. I told her that I was broke but she said, "I got you and Dre, what time y'all picking me up?" I told her that I would call Dre and get back to her. Once I found Dre, I told him what Kat said about treating us and he was cool with it. I called her back and told her that we would be there around one o'clock that afternoon.

Dre met me at M's and we rode together to pick up Kat. She was waiting for us outside of her apartment building. That was a little odd; we usually had to wait for her. Dre got into the backseat and I drove to the Chesapeake in Greenbelt, Maryland. When we got to the door Dre saw his cousin DeeDee. We gave her a hug and introduced her to Kat. No love there, this seemed to tick her off. After getting settled and placing our order - all you could eat crab legs and a pitcher of beer - we seemed to be having a good time. Then Kat asked if Dre and I had any money. I told her, "No, we thought you were treating."

"I was treating after the way you treated me during our relationship."

Dre and I look at each other and back at her like she was crazy. We started arguing, but I calmed down because I realized that we were in PG County and the police out there didn't play. When the waitress brought the check, Kat asked, "What happens if you don't pay for your food? Do they make you wash the dishes?"

The waitress pointed to the police car at the entrance. "They lock you up and charge you with shoplifting."

Dre looked nervous. "Roarke, what are we going to do?" I told Dre not to worry; I had a back-up plan. "Follow me." I got the check, paid for the meal, and walked out. I was pissed; I couldn't believe she tried to get back at me. I told Dre to pick up the pace because I saw her coming out the door from the corner of my eye, laughing and yelling, "I'll make y'all sorry asses pay, tell me I ain't a bad bitch." I was thinking I'm going to have the last laugh. I pulled off and went to the carwash across the street. She was yelling across the street, "Roarke, you better take me back home," but I didn't care how she got home. She tried to make a fool out of me and she didn't know whom she was messing with. I left her at least fifty miles from home; this was before the subway was put in that neighborhood. So she was shit out of luck.

I didn't see or hear from her for two months and then she left a message on my answering machine. "Roarke, it's not over, I will get you." I started hiding my car because I knew she was capable of some treacherous things.

After a few minutes, I went back outside and checked my car; my back window was on the seat. Damn, Damn, Damn. I called the police the next morning to make a report for the insurance company. They asked if I knew who did it and I told them no thinking hopefully that this would make us even now and Kat would leave me alone for good. My mother was speechless. "Who would do this to you?" I told her it was Kat. "I told you that girl was trash, she doesn't know any better." I went to work with my broken window and I could

what i do is
TABOO

hear all the whispers. "What happened to Roarke?" I was really feeling the strain of being single. I know it was time to settle down and have a family. Good-bye streets, it's time for me to ride away in the sunset.

I realized that in order to start a new life with Tessa I needed a new job, so I applied for everything I could find. I finally got a call from the National Naval Medical Center in Bethesda, Maryland. I took the job and would start in two weeks.

Since I had a new job it was time to move out of M's house. I was looking forward to having my own place, but was also scared because women were my weakness and I knew that too many temptations would make me slip.

I found an apartment at Iverson Towers, directly across the street from Sam's Carwash. My apartment was completely laid out; I got everything from the Barbershop, even my Persian rugs. I had a friend of mine come in to redo the bath area. He added a shower seat and a massaging showerhead and made it lower to be used while sitting or standing. Tessa's parents wouldn't let her move in with me until we were married; we still had nine months to go. It was hard. As much as I loved Tessa, being in the apartment alone was grueling.

Dre, Reggie, Darnell, and I took a bus to Pennsylvania for a ski trip. None of us could ski but we went for the parties. The hotel offered all you could drink parties, pool parties, and pajama parties; everything a single person needed.

On the second day there was a pool party and one of the games was using ping-pong balls. There were teams of two. One person had to stuff ping-pong balls into their bathing suit and the other person had to take them out using only their mouth. This one couple got carried away. The guy removed twenty-two ping-pong balls from the girl's swimsuit, but continued to search her bikini bottom for more balls. He was licking her and eventually the bottoms came off. Dre and Reggie got a lot of pictures.

The next night there was a pajama party. I wore silk boxers with a tank top. When we got to the hall there was a couple on the floor slobbering each other down. She stopped, came over to Dre, and started to blow him. The girl's boyfriend was cursing at Dre, but Reggie and Darnell grabbed him before he could get close. Dre was getting the blowjob of his life. She was sucking him so hard it felt like she was sucking on me, too. Dre came all over her face while the boyfriend watched. I felt bad about that but the girl walked up to Dre.

The DJ was jamming and everyone was getting freaked. Then the DJ made an announcement. "Ladies, go to the Classic Ballroom on the third floor and gentlemen, make your way down the hall to the Vintage Ballroom."

I went back to my room to get some single dollar bills and by the time I got back to the Ballroom the first stripper was already on the floor. She only had two dollars, and when she came to me I put five one-dollar bills into her garter. She did a handstand and put her backside on my lap. I played with her for a little while then she flipped back over and thanked me.

The next stripper came out and I realized I knew her. Her name was Ebony and she was an old friend of Shake's. She came over and gave me a hug. I put ten dollars in her garter and she gave me a lap dance. Other guys kept grabbing her breasts so she turned around and sat on me for ten minutes. She asked if I was the only one with money and I said, "Yeah."

She said, "The other strippers are going to take real good care of you!"

The next stripper, Diamond, was on her way out and Ebony let her know about me. She headed straight for me, pulled me out of the chair, and laid me on the floor. I put

what i do is
TABOO

dollar bills all around me as far as I could reach. The other strippers came out and pulled down my shorts and took turns riding and sucking my dick. Diamond was holding me down and the fellas were going crazy.

Then came Sunshine; she was exquisite. She pushed the other girls aside and slithered down on me like she was the bun and I was the hotdog. She spun around on my manhood and then started to contract her pussy like they were pliers. I was in heaven. She jumped up and I came like a broken water pipe. The strippers ran over and licked me dry. It was so nice to be me and my boy Dre got it all on tape. I think I can now make the Guinness Book of World Records for best live sex show.

Unusual places:

These are some of the unusual places that I have had sex: at the park on the sliding board in the woods; in the sky lift at King's Dominion night club during happy hour; at the strip club; in the rain; on a balcony; in a swimming pool; in the water at the beach and in the lifeguard chair; on the bus going to Atlantic City; the subway; a metro bus; in the bathroom at work; on the spirit of Washington ship; in the backseat of the car while Dre was driving; and in the bedroom at Angelo's while everybody watched.

Back to the story:

On the bus ride home I was dreaming about being in my own bed. I woke to a commotion in the back of the bus and I heard Dre's name. When I got to the back of the bus, I saw Dre screwing this girl's brains out in the bathroom. The fellas were cheering him on. Each time a playa puts down his black book another playa is born and the saga continues on and on. So Dre has picked up the book along with the keys to The

Zone. After realizing Dre wasn't fighting I went back to my seat and started a conversation with the lady seated beside me. She asked if I was in a committed relationship. I said, "Yes, in my mind but not my body." She asked me to explain and I told her about Tessa and my plans for our future, but those plans were in jeopardy because my body had a mind of its own.

"So what you're saying is your mind is hers but your dick belongs to the world."

"Yes," I replied, "in a nutshell. I have truly been naughty this weekend. Before I met this girl it was no big deal to cheat, but now I feel guilty." The woman and I had a nice conversation and then I fell back asleep.

When we got back to the parking lot in Capital Heights, I went to my mother's house. I knocked on the door. Even though I had keys, I had to respect her privacy. She looked out over the balcony. "Do you have your key?" I nodded. "Well use it and come on in." I went downstairs to the basement and she yelled, "Boy, what are you doing in my basement?" I told her I was just reminiscing. Boy, if these walls could talk.

I went upstairs to my mother's bedroom and told her about my trip. I told her about everything, the pool party, pajama party, and the strippers. I actually felt ashamed.

She said, "Roarke, you need to pull up. It's time for you to quit it, I mean it right now." She wasn't pleased about my trip and I never wanted to make my mother mad. I stayed for a little while longer and then went home.

When I got to my building, there were women everywhere, probably for some convention. I got on the elevator with a group of women and all at once they introduced themselves to me. I kept silent until I got to my floor and jumped out. When I reached my door, I heard a soft, sweet voice say, "You never told me your name."

what i do is
TABOO

I turned and saw one of the young ladies from the elevator. "They call me Roarke. What's your name?"

"My name is Candy; you've never had anything this sweet."

As much as I wanted to have this conversation, I knew that I shouldn't, so I said, "It was nice meeting you," and ran into my apartment.

I loved daiquiris so I pulled out my blender and made a batch of strawberry daiquiris and jumped into the shower. While I was enjoying my relaxing shower my pager was going off and the phone was ringing off the hook. While I was getting out of the shower, I heard a knock at the door. I ran to open it and there stood Candy. She opened her robe and walked into my apartment. "Do you like my bathing suit?"

"Umm, yeah, it's nice." I went back to the bathroom and got myself together. When I got to the living room, she was still there. "Why are you showing me your bathing suit in February?"

She said, "Don't you recognize my suit, Roarke?"

While I was pondering the situation and wondering how to proceed, she walked into the bathroom and locked the door. *What type of shit is this?* I thought. I banged on the door yelling for her to get out and heard the shower on full blast. I opened the door and peeked in the shower and she had the showerhead between her legs. I couldn't move; I was frozen. When she finished she got dressed and left. Later I looked on the floor and saw that she had left a fifty-dollar bill under my door. I guess someone else loved my shower just as much as I did.

I started my new job that Tuesday in a building called The Tower. It had twenty floors and I was surrounded by a new group of single women. This job was very demanding and that was good. My life was going great and I had seven more months before the big day. I hadn't had any incidents since the ski trip and that was a record for me. Tessa asked her parents if she could spend the weekend with me. I was so excited I got off early that Friday to clean and make sure that everything was in order in my apartment.

When Tessa arrived, I took her bags and gave her a hug and kiss. We sat in the living room and talked for a while. She walked over to the bookcase. "Roarke, I didn't know you liked to read." I told her that I had been reading since age four and that one day I planned to write a book about the wild days I had in the hood. She turned and asked, "What type of wild things did you do?" I said, "If I tell you, I'll have to kill you." She started to laugh and I told her, "Some things I have to keep in the vault." I asked her a few questions about her past. But like most females she changed the subject. "So, who is your favorite author?"

"I like them all," I said and began to name a few. "Vera Kohlheim and Saundra Harris, but my all-time favorite is Michael Eric Dyson, that brother is so deep. His research is better than a historian at the Smithsonian Museum."

When the doorbell rang I acted like I didn't hear it. Tessa looked at me like I was crazy. "Roarke, the doorbell is ringing, aren't you going to answer it?" I shrugged my shoulders because I didn't have an answer for her.

Tessa frowned then opened the door and Candy came in with her lace panty set. "Roarke, I really enjoyed the other night. I've never cum like that and it was worth the fifty dollars." Tessa slammed the door and Candy turned around. "Oh, I didn't know you had company."

Tessa looked at me with tears in her eyes and I tried to explain. "It's not what you think."

I grabbed Candy and told her to explain, but she just stared at me and said, "What you gonna do if I don't?" Before

I could say anymore, Tessa had Candy on the floor beating her. Finally Candy started to yell the truth. "I didn't sleep with him! I was trying to entice him but he wouldn't take me."

Tessa hit her again and threw her out into the hallway. "Roarke, is this how it's going to be after we get married? Women throwing themselves at you when I'm not around?"

I finally got her to lie down on the couch and started to give her a gentle massage. I whispered in her ear that I loved her and asked if she wanted to go to dinner and a movie. She agreed and went into the bathroom to freshen up.

We went to Rivertowne, but we weren't into the movie so we went to The Barnside to get something to eat. The waitress took our orders and our food came back fast, but the waitress dropped the food in my lap. I yelled for the manager who came out right away. I explained the situation and he apologized and offered to pay for my dry cleaning. The waitress came back to the table yelling and pushing me. "You don't remember me do you, Roarke?"

I told Tessa it was time to leave and she started to follow me out the door as Kat walked in. She worked at The Barnside and she came in yelling. "Thought I forgot, huh Roarke? It's never over until I say it's over." She slapped me and cut my face with her fake nails. I grabbed her hand before she could hit me again, grabbed Tessa, and ran out the door. Kat and the waitress were standing at the door laughing at us. I was trying to figure out why they weren't chasing us, but that didn't stop me from pulling out of the parking lot like a bat out of hell.

On the way back to my apartment, I asked Tessa if she still wanted to stay and that I wouldn't blame her if she were ready to leave. She said that she would stay until she calmed down.

I turned on the shower and put in a slow jam tape; I didn't want her to see me cry. I was in the shower for a while before she came in and joined me; we made passionate love. As we were getting out of the shower a song came on the radio, *Let Me Love You One More Time* by George Benson. It's about a man who wants to make love to his woman one more time before they break up. I was feeling queasy because what happened to my Jodeci song? I wanted to marry this girl. I started babbling about how much I wanted and needed her. I even called on the name of Jesus to help me. What was going on? Wasn't she the one? Tessa put her clothes on, grabbed her bag, and waved good-bye.

The End

what i do is
TABOO

Acknowledgments and Thanks

Thanks God for allowing me your grace and mercy. To Kayla and lil Rodney, thank you for loaning Daddy to the world if just for a moment. Thank you to my "Earth Angel" or "Angel on Loan" as I call her: my wife Judy. From the day we hooked up to having those wonderful children and all the fun in between, you've truly been a Godsend. I owe God big time for sending you to me.

Thanks to everybody from Barry Farms; Darrell Barnes, Ms. Hainsworth, Curtis, Todd One, Tracey Hardaway, and The Briscoe's.

Thanks to 23rd Street: Calvin, Keith W, Keith E, Tyrone, Ike, Derek, Black Mike, Mr. Jacks Barbershop, Mr. Jack, Kevin Brown, and Eugene Brown.

My running partner Anthony Adams; we ran the city. To Jimmy Twitty, thanks for helping me with my spirituality and for changing with me, you are a true friend. States, I am proud of you. I want to thank David Thomas my friend and business partner. Special thanks to Donovan Davis; thanks for the CD. I extend special thanks, in loving memory of Roy Clemons; I love and miss you. A special mention to Gary "Batman" Green and family, love y'all. And to my very special readers – Michelle Pope, Kia Braxton, Sonya Steedly, Donna Douglas, Stinka, Myrtis Robinson, Antoinette Ray Andrea Adams, and Shelly Gibbs.

Detra Britt Williams, www.detrabrittwilliams.com the baddest gospel singer I know. Thanks to some dynamite writers that helped me: Saundra Harris, Candace Simmons, Vera Kohlheim, Kwame Alexander, and Shana Yarborough. My wonderful editors, Vernetta Johnson, who kept my story straight, and Lisa D'Angelo of www.bookink.com

Thanks to Deborah Charles for getting my writing mind flowing and Ms. Netta B in L Enfant Plaza, thanks for all your encouragement and words of wisdom.

I would like to thank my family, Marsha, Ruth, Robyn, Ronda, and Rocky, Maurice Big Mo' Burden, Kristin, Melvin, Christopher, Brian, Robert Harrison III, Michael, Adrienne, Elaine, and Pete. Life has been a blast being a part of this family; I love all y'all. Thanks to my wonderful sister in-law Dodie Thomas, and Margaret and Joseph Dorsey, the best mother- and father-in-law short of heaven.

A special thanks to my mother, Rojena Bumbry. I could write a million pages about how much I love and miss you. Thank you for always keeping me straight, whether it was taking my car or just sharing some much needed wisdom. Lord knows I needed it. Thanks to my father, Robert Harrison Sr. Dad, I always thought I needed more from you as a father, but time has taught me you gave me just what I needed. You met me where I was and gave me what I needed. I love and miss you.

If I forgot anybody, charge it to me. Just forget it and be big enough to understand. IT'S NOT ABOUT YOU!